Crossing Kansas

Diane Leatherman

This book is based on people and incidents from my life.
However, some events and characters are a product
of my imagination, so the story must be considered a work of
fiction. All names of family members, acquaintances,
and places have been changed.

Copyright © 1998 by Diane Leatherman

Requests for permission to make copies of any part of the
work should be mailed to:
Box 315, Cabin John, MD 20818-0315

ISBN 0-9665861-0-7

Cover fabric art by Diane Leatherman
Printed in the United States of America

*To my friends
who encouraged me,
especially Bunny and John
who made me believe.*

Prologue

It was 1922, two years after women won the vote, when Jerry Jones and Nancy Hall ran away to get married. Nancy was a sophomore in high school and she was sure she could improve her life if she got away from her parents. She told them she was going to spend the night with a girl friend, packed a small bag, went with Jerry to a justice of the peace in a nearby town, and got married.

While their own house was being built by her father and paid for by his father, they lived with Jerry's family in a big house, filled with his brothers and sisters.

It was an awful experience for Nancy; no one could have come up to her high standards, and her mother-in-law didn't come near. She hung sheets out on the clothesline that the younger children had wet, without washing them, and served the family canned peaches. No one in Nancy's family had ever done those things.

Nancy went home to cry on her mother's shoulder when Jerry's sisters borrowed her clothes without asking, or when Jerry went out to a basketball game or a square dance without her, or when he brought his friends to their home for a party and they all drank and smoked. Nancy didn't and was left with the mess to clean up.

Nancy's mother, who was annoyed with her hardheaded daughter, answered, "You made your bed, now you lie in it." So Nancy decided that if you cannot lick them, you should join them and took up drinking and smoking herself. She was careful, though, to not become an alcoholic; she never drank before 5 p.m.

Jerry Jones' father owned the bank where Jerry worked as a teller. The bank went under in 1927 a little earlier than most, thanks to a rumor spread by a relative, and everything the Jones owned was sold on the courthouse steps, even the quilts that had been wedding gifts. Jerry and Nancy moved from Grain Valley to Kansas City with $30 and a toddler named Jeannie.

In the city Jerry Jones found a job selling automobiles. They were more fortunate than many, he had always been fascinated by automobiles, having several at any time in various states of apartness in his family's yard. And there definitely was a future in selling cars.

PART ONE

Chapter One

Ten years later on a December day in 1937, a nun walked into Nancy Jones' hospital room, as she was awakening from twilight sleep, and asked, "Would you like to see your beautiful baby girl?"

"What little girl?" asked Nancy Jones, who had been expecting a boy this time.

At age 34, Nancy was quite old to be having another child but a boy would be a link with Jerry; what good would another girl be? Dr. Donlan had assured her in late pregnancy that the heartbeat indicated a boy. Jerry loved the manly sports of hunting and fishing. If they had a boy, Jerry could teach him to hunt and fish and would be grateful to Nancy for the opportunity.

When her husband came to visit that evening she apologized to him, "I'm sorry I had another girl."

"It's better this way," he assured her. "Girls aren't as much trouble as boys." Besides, he thought to himself, now that he was little older it might be kind of fun to have daddy's little girl. Nancy and Jerry had been teenagers when their first daughter, Jean, was born. Babies were of no interest to him then.

Jerry also said, "Jean really misses you. I'll bring her in tomorrow."

The Jones' older daughter was not quite 14 and a little tearful. It was two days before Christmas when she came with her father to visit her mother at St. Joseph's Hospital.

After a day to reconcile with having another daughter, Nancy shared with them that she was thinking about naming the baby after two favorite aunts of hers, Georgia and Virginia. "We could call her Georgie Jen."

"Daddy, you promised me I could name the baby!" Jean burst out. No sister of hers was going to be named Georgie Jen. Indeed he had promised her, searching for a way to make up to Jean for the fact that her mother would be in the hospital for two weeks during the holidays.

So Jean had named her sister Linda. At least it wasn't Barbara Ann; there were five Barbara Anns already in the hospital nursery.

Nancy had given up so much, maybe it wouldn't be that hard to give up Georgie Jen also.

◆ ◆ ◆

Jerry was doing well enough financially now that they were able to move from their apartment and pay cash for a brick home with a screened-in front porch, two fireplaces, and a knotty pine paneled recreation room in the basement.

Chapter Two

"Mom, goddammit, get her out of here!" Jean was trying to play her new record, "In the Mood," for her friends. Jean's temper was something to be feared, but she had come by it honestly. Usually she was more gentle with her little sister than she was with anyone else. Although Nancy and Jerry felt they had always sacrificed to make sure that Jean had everything necessary and then some, it was difficult for Jean, whose childhood had been constricted by small, shared apartments, to see that Linda knew nothing about not getting what she wanted.

Linda was such a friendly little thing with a smile almost always on her face; Nancy said, "Linda's never met a stranger," knowing that appearances were important and certainly Linda was a little picture.

◆ ◆ ◆

The country went to war and Jean went off to college. All of the young men were gone and what else was there for a young woman to do? She made up her mind a week before school started. It was the same school chosen by her neighborhood friend, Taffy. Nancy threw herself into last minute preparations, buying, ironing, and packing the trunk that had belonged to Aunt George. Jean and Taffy took the train to Oklahoma.

Two weeks after they left, Jean's parents received a tear-stained letter that asked, "Please come get me." They packed the car and drove to Oklahoma and found their daughter settled in. Jean got a kick out of showing off her cute baby sister Linda to the girls in the dorm, and then the Jones' drove home.

In her sister's absence, Linda made friends with the next door neighbors. The Swallows had made sure that the Jones' understood when they moved in, "We don't like children."

Linda toddled over and plucked the heads from the tulips lining the Swallows' front walk. It was the beginning of a lovely friendship.

Oddly enough, the Swallows seemed to understand some of a child's needs. They had crayons, paper, and time. They would offer Linda a choice, "Would you like to build a swing or go to Fairyland Amusement Park?"

Nancy was too busy keeping a perfect house for such things and, besides, she didn't drive.

Actually, Nancy had once known how, learning to drive her grandfather around the farm fields as a fourteen-year-old, where he supervised the field work as a gentleman, first on horseback and later from the automobile.

But after she was married, Jerry had complained about her driving one time too many.

"Fine, then you can do it yourself!" she shouted as she slammed the keys down on the table and never drove again.

◆ ◆ ◆

Mrs. MacMillan, the elderly neighbor on the other side, was stout and unable to move around with Linda but she sat in her wicker rocker on her front porch and they played word games. One day they were playing "In My Garden I have..." when Linda said, "My flower begins with an f."

"Linda, phlox doesn't begin with a f," Mrs. MacMillan gently corrected the child.

"I don't mean phlox; I mean fiolets."

Mr. MacMillan, a Scotsman, came home and said to her, "Good evening, little kettle."

Linda wondered aloud to her mother, "Why, since he is almost old, does Mr. Mac talk baby talk?"

Linda confided to Mrs. MacMillan that when she grew up, "I am going to have five or seven children."

She began to wish that she would find a baby that no one wanted. "I would bring it home and keep it in a box in the corner of my room and not let it bother Mama and Daddy." She often fantasized caring for her baby as she fell asleep at night, on the nights when she was not telling herself a story about Indians and pioneers.

◆ ◆ ◆

After two years Jean came home. In college she had learned to wear blue jeans, smoke, and call colored people "darkies."

Nancy said to her daughter, "It isn't okay to call colored persons darkies." She liked the blue jeans so much that she got some for herself and wore them every day.

Linda knew two colored people: Cleo, the woman who cleaned for her mother, and Richard, who worked for her father at the auto dealership and drove a car out to take Linda and her mother downtown, twice a year, to purchase Linda's clothes for the coming season.

On these downtown shopping trips they would go up the elevator to the fifth floor of Harzfeld's Department Store, where Mrs. Wolff would say, "I have some dresses that I've put aside; they are perfect for Linda."

Miss Lee would x-ray Linda's feet in the new shoes, to make sure they fit properly. Linda would peer in the eye piece at the top of the machine and wiggle her toes hello to herself.

◆ ◆ ◆

At night, Linda snuggled back in her father's lap and suggested, "Let's listen to 'Mr. District Attorney.'"

Jean asked, "Daddy, can I go on to more school?"

Jerry Jones thought that college was really wasted on girls, "You'll get married and your husband will support you. Although I think it's a good idea for girls to learn to type and take shorthand because you never know..."

"Daddy, I hate typing. I'm good at math and I like to draw..." Later that week, Jean landed a job as a secretary.

Linda was delighted to have her big sister back from college. "Let's listen to Harry James on the radio," she said as she watched Jean put pin curls in her hair at night, carefully putting two bobby pins in each curl, one this way, one that.

She watched, horrified, while her sister, holding a piece of cotton with nail polish remover on it, lit a cigarette. The remover caught fire and sent a flame up in front of her sister's face. "Daddy, Daddy..." both girls screamed.

◆ ◆ ◆

Linda started to school herself, a promising little thing who tried her very best to please the teachers.

After school, Linda dreamt of playing the piano. Linda cut out paper keys and laid them out on the coffee table, where she sat playing. Nancy told Jerry, "Linda is so strange, she thinks she has a friend named Jarett. She plays a piano that's not there. It worries me."

When Linda's class went to the Municipal Auditorium to hear the symphony orchestra, Linda mounted large productions of dancers and musicians in her head.

Her mother told her father, "I think it's time for piano lessons. A new piano would look good in the living room."

"My god, Nancy, do you think money grows on trees?" But Jerry let her buy the cherry wood George Steck spinet.

Linda was afraid of her piano teacher. Miss Lawson, a spinster, demanded perfection of her pupils' fingers and minds. She had her pupils learn their pieces backwards as well as forwards. She was like Linda's mother who always said, "There's no point in doing something unless you do it right."

It helped, after her lesson, to have Daddy take her to Spencer's Drugstore, where he gave her a nickel and she could buy a pack of gum to cram in her mouth, one piece after the other, and chew out some of the anxiety.

◆ ◆ ◆

Linda stated her goal in life, "I want to grow up to look just like Jean."

It didn't do Jean much good, though, to look so great when there weren't any young men around.

Jean told her parents, "Taffy and I and some other girls are going to Ft. Leonard Wood on Friday."

These weekend trips in search of young men worried her parents but Jerry told Nancy, "She's a grown young woman now, with a job, and can do as she pleases."

Nancy worried about what the neighbors would think but Jerry said, "All of the young people are doing the same thing." He didn't know about the time that his daughter woke up the next morning in a BOQ.

Linda watched her mother and sister make batches of brownies. Her mother packed them really well so that they could travel around the globe to Jean's young men friends, who all went overseas.

Jean found one young man and their song was "You'll Never Walk Alone." He went off to war as a pilot and was shot down by an Italian convoy over the Mediterranean. Linda knew that her sister was very sad.

To Linda, the war meant going into the basement at school during air raid drills or sitting on her father's lap on the front porch during a blackout, listening for the block warden to come walking past, greeting everyone. She missed the fine point that the block warden was a first generation German immigrant; she played "war" with the other children and everyone knew that the enemy was called "Japs." She carried cans of grease or bundles of newspaper to school for the war effort and watched her mother count out coupons from the ration book. She had no idea the war had any connection with the orange powder her mother worked into the oleo as she gave Linda a piece of the fat to suck.

The second young man Jean found also went off to war and was shot, but just in the leg. Jean was so happy, "He can come home and he won't have to go back." Jean said his name was Jim Jeff.

When he could walk with crutches, he came from the hospital in Springfield to visit Jean's family. "Are you Jean's sista'?" he asked the attractive Nancy Jones when she answered the front door.

Jim Jeff was from Talladega, Alabama, and Linda listened and carefully copied his "yes, mam" which came out like "yowsome." He always said "mam" and "sir" to everyone. He was so handsome in his uniform that she tried to steal him away from her big sister, posing in her most fetching, seven-year-old manner. But Jim Jeff remained true to Jean and asked her, "Will you marry me, Suga'?"

Jerry and Nancy Jones invited all of their friends from Kansas City to the wedding in the Army chapel, close to the hospital in Springfield. Everyone went back to the hotel after the wedding to enjoy dinner and champagne. They were able to give Jean and Jim Jeff a nice celebration because that year the war was over and cars were once again being manufactured. Auto dealers sold every car before it even came off of the line in Detroit. Some people waited on lists for years before they received their cars. Jerry and his partner made a million dollars.

They could have joined a country club but Nancy and Jerry couldn't see any point in that; they also turned down the opportunity to send their younger daughter to private school. Nancy said, "Linda's doing fine in school; she doesn't have any problems."

Linda carried the slick, coated sales brochure for Chrysler-Plymouth to school and sold a car to her third grade teacher. The Sales Manager bought her a box of chocolates.

Linda had learned to hate and fear the times when grownups drank. She knew her mother would always drink too much and forget that Linda even existed. After the wedding was worse than most times because everyone drank too much. Linda told the drunken wedding photographer, "If you take my picture I am going to throw a goblet at you."

She was sent off to bed by her parents.

She was unsure how long she had been asleep when she heard her parents come to bed very late after the wedding celebration and Mama was screaming "Oh Jerry!" and sobbing. It was like a bad dream.

Linda thought her father was hurting her mother somehow and made up her mind, "I'll never let anyone make me feel that way. I'll stop loving them."

Fortunately her parents didn't drink every night, just on social occasions and trips. Those were the only times it was so horrible that she had to hold her breath, stop living, and wait for time to pass.

But every summer there were trips. One summer they traveled all over the south, where they met Jim Jeff's relatives, some of whom had big, beautiful homes because they were wealthy and some who lived in reduced but genteel circumstances. One of these homes had windows so tall on the second floor that they could have served as doors, but to nowhere. Jean said, "I'm afraid of sleepwalking through the windows and falling."

It became Linda's goal to count how many bathrooms there were in each home as they visited it or to watch for chimneys without houses that stood as Sherman's sentinels, while they crossed the southern states.

Other summers they went west because her parents felt,

"Why would you want to go east? That's where all of the people are." Her parents also said, "Crossing Kansas is hell. There are no clean restrooms or restaurants and it is always so damn hot!"

They were fortunate because, since Jerry was a car dealer, they had one of the first automobile air conditioners. It looked like the tank of a vacuum cleaner inserted at the top of the window on the passenger side. They would pack it full of dry ice and the air blew through the tank to cool the car. It was a little better than flying fast across Kansas with the car windows down and all of the hot, dry, wind blowing in. Linda could count on her father putting in a hard day of driving eighty or ninety miles an hour across Kansas and stopping at 5 or 6 p.m. It was Denver or bust. The drive was followed by clean up at the motel and the cocktail hour, which lasted a good deal longer than any hour. Sometimes it was quite late when they went to dinner.

Linda thought, "Maybe if I begin to whine we will go to dinner sooner, and Mama won't get drunk," although she had never seen her mother drink without getting drunk.

"Can we go eat now, I'm hungry. Please let's go eat. It's late!" This plan never worked but Linda became quite accomplished at whining.

◆ ◆ ◆

For a while after the wedding, Jean and Jim Jeff lived with Linda and her parents and Jim Jeff went to law school on the GI bill. Jean supported them by working as a secretary. When they moved to their own apartment, Linda asked, "Why is Jim Jeff taking Jean away?"

Linda missed her sister terribly and began to work on her own hope chest for when she would get married. Jean and Jim Jeff teased her, "Linda has a hopeless chest."

But Linda's mother taught her how to sew so that she could embroider dish towels, pillow cases, and finger tip guest towels with fringed edges. "Just three strands and you knot it like so..." said Nancy. "You could catch your big toe in this stitch!" she said as she ripped out Linda's stitches.

One day Linda heard her mother say that Jean was going to have a baby! Out the back door and down the block she ran with this absolutely wonderful news...at last a baby in the family.

After the baby's birth, her sister came from a week's stay in the hospital to her parents' home. They had hired a nurse to help Nancy care for the baby and Jean. Nancy had made an organdy skirt with a huge blue satin bow and lining for the wicker bassinet. Jean had pink satin mules to match her robe. Everything was just right, except the baby. He cried a lot and turned his face away from Jean when she put him to her breast. So they decided to put him on formula and Jean was pretty sure he didn't like her. No one would let Linda near the baby. At 11 years of age, they thought she was too young.

One night when no one was around, the baby started to cry. Linda changed his diaper and rocked him and sang to him and knew for the first time that she loved someone. His name was Tommy, but his grandfather would call him "Ike" because of his pale crewcut and broad grin.

He was joined three years later by a sister and then, in a couple of years, another one. Jim Jeff called from the hospital and said, "They ran out of boys so they gave us a girl with red hair."

The children became the most important people in Linda's life. She would clean, scrub, and baby sit free just to be with them. Jerry asked, "Don't you think you might wear out your welcome at your sister's house?"

"Oh no, Daddy, I work hard." The only bad part was when Jim Jeff beat Tommy. He was still sitting in a baby feeding table when Jim Jeff would grab him out and hit him with a belt for not eating. People had only pled with Linda to eat. It was so painful to see her beloved baby beaten.

Jean didn't seem very happy to be a mother; it was hard for her to get organized. Little piles of clothes lay about and the dirty dishes never seemed to end. Perhaps, after all, she welcomed Linda's help.

One day, when someone knocked on the front door and Jean was alone with the children, she ran to the furthermost room and hid in a corner, afraid and bewildered. Crying, she called her mother. Nancy called a taxi and came right to her daughter's home. Jean couldn't go into crowds. She felt her behavior was out of her control; all strange situations were frightening. For a while, like her mother, she gave up driving; and then, when she resumed she only drove within her community, never out on the highway. Once Jean had to leave Linda at the doctor's office with the baby because she just could not stay. Linda felt so proud when the doctor's staff thought that Kathy was her baby.

Finally, one day when Linda was thirteen or fourteen, she told her sister, "I hate it when you or Jim Jeff beat Tommy." Jean burst into tears.

Chapter Three

"Damn you, God, you better make me grow up right now! You've already made me wait too long."

Linda matured slowly. She would lie by the window at night and demand that God give her breasts and a period.

Women were surrounded by the most wonderful secrets and she was locked out. Jean went into the bathroom and closed the door and did secret things. Linda didn't feel as if it was a sorority that she would grow into; she just felt flat and ignorant and very angry with God for putting her into this position. She blamed grownups for the ignorant part. She knew there was some kind of conspiracy to keep her from the knowledge that it seemed everyone else had.

"Is that something Linda shouldn't see?" her mother would ask. Linda found a fake coin that her father had taken from his pocket. On the front of the coin was a couple dressed in evening dress. The young lady was chic and perched on spike heels. The man was old, shorter than the woman, leering, and appeared to be loaded with money. On the back of the coin, the man had lifted the woman's skirt and had his hand between her legs. Linda was pretty sure that this was one of those things that "Linda shouldn't see." She knew better than to ask and came to some conclusions of her own. When she played with her dolls, she acted out a scene where the young beautiful doll was pursued by a male. This required imagination because she had no male dolls and the bodies of the girl dolls were not mature. The story she told herself was all pursuit. Linda didn't know what to do after the pursued was caught. She was pretty sure it was anti-climactic because, at that point, the girl doll lost all of her power.

There were also things Linda shouldn't hear. When Tommy was born, a visiting friend had asked Nancy, "Are they going to circumcise the baby?"

Linda asked, "What does circumcise mean?"

Nancy evaded her daughter's question but the visiting friend told her, "The doctors cut a little piece of skin off the end of the baby's penis." Linda felt grateful for the information.

It wasn't so much that Nancy didn't believe in sex education; it was more a matter that she didn't believe in sex. She ignored it; it didn't exist, until of course it did.

Then, ten days before Linda turned fifteen, her periods started. Her chest was still flat but at last God had proved he was working on it. The following summer she had her hair cut and her braces taken off. Her father, on his way to pick her up, drove right past her. That was good news; it meant to her that she looked grown up.

"Daddy, Daddy, it's me," she called loudly a couple of times before her father heard her. Her father pulled over and she hopped in the car. And the two of them, riding in the same car, had no idea what to say to each other. Suddenly she was pretty sure that she was an attractive young woman and she might be able to handle the script with boys her own age, but she hadn't the least notion what one should say to fathers at this point. Her father, for his part, recognized two kinds of women, ladies and others. He didn't know what fathers say to attractive, fifteen-year-old daughters.

Linda began to try to sew some of her own clothes; it was actually a revolt of sorts. Linda bought the materials with her own baby-sitting money and then closed her bedroom door so that she could cut out the pattern. Her mother yelled out, "Don't you cut into that expensive material; you don't know what you are doing."

Linda cut anyway, in secret. Usually the results were

unsatisfactory to Linda and she thought that she was probably just hard-headed like her daddy said and sloppy like her mother said.

For years, Linda had said, "I don't like boys." They had seemed to return the feeling. Then, all of a sudden, boys started to call on the phone. There was a Gary and a Jack. At last she was part of the sorority; she had the power. She didn't stay home one night the summer she was sixteen.

Her parents bought a split level home in the J. D. Michaels section of Kansas City so that, "Linda can meet a higher class boy."

J. D. Michaels created beautiful residential areas in the south part of the city. No clotheslines, trash cans, Jewish or colored home buyers were allowed. Beautiful artwork was imported from other countries and many blocks boasted sculpture, fountains, pillars or tilework.

Her best friend in the new high school was Marie. Marie was Catholic like Linda always wanted to be. When they spent the night with each other, the two girls knelt down beside the bed, one black curly head and one ash blond, to say their prayers before going to sleep; Marie's prayers always lasted longer. Linda went through her short repertoire: the Lord's Prayer, the beatitudes and a psalm or two. Marie was still praying.

Linda told Marie, "I am thinking about becoming a nurse." She even took a hospital tour at St. Mary's, a tour designed for teens who were considering nursing as a profession.

Her mother said, "Nursing isn't very ladylike." Linda let that idea go.

There were sororities in the new high school. Friends of Nancy and Jerry Jones saw to it that Linda was invited to some of the pledge parties during the summer. Marie and Linda pledged the same sorority, which had special colors: purple and yellow. The pledges had to wear them on meeting day and carry cigar boxes full of candy for their members.

Some of the members yelled at the pledges or said very mean things quietly like, "I don't know why we ever pledged such an ugly girl as you." After they were initiated and learned the secret phrases, their sorority sisters tried to get them to smoke, but Marie and Linda closed their mouths tightly when their sorority sisters tried to put cigarettes between their lips.

Every time Linda's father walked into the bathroom after her, he accused her, "You've been smoking in here." It was impossible for him to believe that she would choose not to smoke on her own; he was pretty sure that he would need to save her. He himself had just recently quit, when the first hints came out that cancer and smoking might be linked. He didn't want to die of cancer.

Linda said to her father, "I want a car."

"No, I don't believe in such things," her father said at first.

Then, before she had gotten her license, he ordered a yellow convertible with a white continental kit for her from the factory.

"My God, Jerry, have you lost your mind?"

Linda didn't wait for her father to answer her mother. She ran to the kitchen to call Marie. On the last day of her sophomore year, she drove the car to school. After school her friends rode with her in the convertible with the top down, to the drive-in. A carful of boys followed them into and out of the drive-in and, when Linda stopped at the corner, the boys couldn't stop in time. They were watching the girls and ran into the connie kit. They got out of their car and came to the driver's window to talk to Linda.

"Don't tell me who you are. My daddy owns a Chrysler-Plymouth dealership and he can fix it," Linda told the boys.

Their car was old and they came from East High; it looked to Linda like they didn't have much money and now, since she wouldn't let them tell her, she could honestly tell her father, "I don't know who ran into the car."

But her father knew the man who owned the gas station on that corner and he called him, just in case he might have seen anything.

"Sure, the boys got out and talked to the girls," the gas station owner told her father, who was disappointed and hurt that Linda had not told him the truth.

Linda tried to explain, "Daddy, we have plenty of money to fix the car and those boys don't have any."

To her parents' consternation, Linda proceeded to meet and date boys from other parts of town and not from the new high school in the better part of Kansas City. She settled with Wesley for the last two years of high school. His mother was a single parent. Wesley and his mom had little money. He had sort of reared himself while his mother was working to support them. They lived in a tiny apartment in the top of an old house. But Wes was cool; he played black rhythm and blues musicians on his record player, not that silly, white Bill Haley rock 'n roll stuff. Only white kids thought that square stuff was cool. Wesley taught Linda how to dance after she ended up on the floor three times when they first danced together. Once they even won a dance contest.

Many of the kids at Wesley's high school had sex. Some had to get married right after graduation. Linda was mostly unsure about sex but she knew two things: making out felt good and it was bad to go all of the way. Wesley accepted her parameters.

◆ ◆ ◆

The year she was a senior was the first year that a black student was admitted to her high school. Linda noticed that he was all alone and felt sorry for him but he was an eighth grader and a boy and no amount of sympathy would allow her to speak to him.

Once when Aunt George was visiting Linda's mother, Linda said,"If I fall in love with a black man, I will marry him."

Aunt George looked at Mrs. Jones and sputtered, "My God, Nancy, what is that child saying?"

Later Jean said, "Since you know how Aunt George feels, you didn't have to bait her that way; you could just keep your opinions to yourself."

One night, after Linda had babysat with Tommy and his sisters and was spending the night at Jean and Jim Jeff's house, Jean said to her, "Stay awake and keep me company while I nurse the baby and I'll tell you what it's like to have a baby." Jean told Linda about the hypo that makes you feel like you have had several cocktails. "I tried to hold back when the baby was coming because it felt like I was going to go to the bathroom there on the table in front of all those people."

With her own car and dates, Linda had less time for Jean and Jim Jeff's children and soon was old enough to go off to college. She wasn't sure, though, that she wanted to go to college. She often fantasized in French class about having a baby with Wesley, actually two very close in age for starters. They were going to be boys. Then she would have girls next. She thought it was important to not have an only child. She always felt like an only child herself and thought it was awful. Of course they would get married.

When she wasn't thinking about getting married or having children, Linda thought about going far away to college, like back east somewhere, but her daddy said, "No, I don't believe in that. You might get strange if you go back east."

Her high school counselor said, "Forget it; there's no way you could get an adequate scholarship if your father won't give you anything," even though Linda was named to the National Honor Society.

Wesley, one year ahead of her, had gone north to school, where he had received a scholarship. She thought for a while about going to Wesley's school but then by summer she couldn't stand him.

She finally decided, more or less by default, to go to a

small girls' junior college in the middle of the state, where her grandmother had gone more than a half century before. The school had been started for daughters of Confederate soldiers. It was in Callaway County, known as little Dixie, which had seceded from the State of Missouri because Missouri would not secede from the Union.

On the long drive to Linda's college, her father pointed out to Linda and his wife the interstate highway that was being constructed across the United States, "The highway and Linda will be finished next year about the same time." Actually, he was wrong in both cases.

Nancy began to drink more often now that her nest was emptying.

Chapter Four

There was a very tall sophomore from the boys' college in town looking over the new girls as they entered South Dormitory. When he saw Linda, he said to the friend with him, "There she is; that's the one." And he set about trying to meet her.

Several people came up to Linda over the next couple of weeks to tell her, "There's a tall Sig Alph who wants a date with you."

Linda had gone away to college resolved to become an independent woman who would have an interesting life. She fantasized having a career and her own apartment in some distant city; her parents would be shocked at the thought of her living alone. While most of the other girls felt homesick and went about in tears for a few days, she didn't at all. She kept her resolve to have an interesting single life until the tall blond Sig Alph named Freddy managed a date with her. It was about three weeks.

October, 1956

Dear Marie,

I have been really busy. You probably have been too but I wanted to write you because I miss you. The building I live in is very old. I can imagine it being here when my grandmother was. It is red brick, has a tower and gingerbread decorating the front porch.

I have been dating one guy named Freddy. He is very tall and different from Wesley. He can't dance and I miss that. Down here after the second date, you might as well be going steady.

I guess I will try to get an AA to teach in grade school because that only takes two years and I want to get out in the world as soon as I can.

The housemothers had a evening meeting the other night and the subject was proper table manners. Can you believe that?

How's Iowa?

Love ya lots,
Linda

P. S. When will you be home for Christmas?

Freddy was slender and rather delicate for all of his height. Linda couldn't really say why things went as they did. "It doesn't feel like a romance from a book," she told her roommate. "It doesn't feel like anything I have control over," she said as she kept dating him. Yet she didn't feel swept away. Freddy seemed strange, at least compared to most of the other fraternity boys, so it was odd to her that she settled in with him. He would do things like yodel or skip in the middle of the street. "I guess you could call him eccentric," she explained to her friends. But he was also lonely; his eccentricity kept him from being accepted by his fraternity brothers. Next to Freddy, Linda was a paragon of experience.

All of the girls had to sign out whenever they went off campus. On Sundays they were required to attend church and wear hats and gloves. It was mandatory to wear dresses each night to dinner and young men were never, ever to go higher than the first floor parlors of the dormitories.

One night in November, Linda's suite mate came in and announced, "The building's on fire."

That was too unbelievable so Linda said to her roommate, "Wake up; there's a fire drill."

They closed the transom, got their towels and slippers, went out into the hall and shut the door. Linda stood at attention outside of the door. "What are you doing?" her roommate asked.

"I'm waiting for the hall proctor to call roll like we're supposed to."

Her roommate grabbed her and pulled her down the narrow back steps that colored help normally used, just as the column of smoke was coming around the corner from the grand front staircase.

Topped by a Victorian tower, the front staircase was going up like a chimney. On the way out, Linda hoped that the fire wouldn't reach the formal closet. All of her formals were there. She had a long red net strapless and a short satin and the formal with bronze spangles and, of course, the requisite half dozen petticoats to go with them.

Out on the street, looking back at the raging flames, Linda thought, "This is probably the only time in my life I will see such a thing." So she sat down on the curb and watched.

Freddy arrived on the scene, didn't see Linda, and borrowed a gas mask from the fire department. He ran in North Hall and across the second floor hall that arched over the driveway and entered South Hall before it fell apart. He was looking for Linda, recognized her room number and entered her room, opened the closet which burst into flame from the rush of air, and came running out carrying an armload of her clothing. He fell panting to the ground.

The pitiful little single town fire engine came up and tried to pump water up from Senior Lake. Before it could, though, the fire could be seen through the windows of all four floors and the majestic four story brick building's front wall parted company with the rest of the walls and fell, almost intact, crashing to the ground.

All night lines of girls waited to call their parents from the phones in the remaining dorms, but most of the families who watched the late news had already seen pictures of the majestic building in flames and were tying up the lines trying to call in.

Nancy was worried but Jerry said, "Goddamit, that's one

of the other buildings." It was like the time when Linda was a little girl and had a temperature of 105. Her father said, "The goddamed thermometer's broken," and that was that.

After she was safely home in Kansas City, Linda's mother said, "To think, Freddy ran into that burning building and he's his parents' only child..." But she also said, "Oh, why did he save this old coat?"

Linda, Jean, and their mother went to Harzfeld's the next day. For once, Nancy didn't have all of the packages delivered to their house. The three were each carrying two or three bags.

As they stood waiting for an elevator, Jean overheard a woman say to her husband, on spying the three so laden with purchases, "A fool and his money..."

Jean, who could put anyone properly in their place, turned to the woman and told her witheringly, "My little sister lost everything in the fire at William Woods College." The three Jones women then stepped into the elevator, while the door closed behind their solidarity.

Since Linda's family was the only family that had adequate insurance coverage, she was the only one who went back to school after Thanksgiving with more than one or two outfits. Her wardrobe became a lending library of clothing. She would often be sewing other girls into their clothes before she was ready for her own date.

In spite of the fire, Linda throve on the opportunities at school. When Jean was in high school she had taught Linda to say "Buenos noches," as they were falling asleep, so Linda rather fancied herself a linguist and had taken both French and Spanish. Jean had often humored her little sister by playing word games. They had even made up secret names for their parents, "Let's call Mama, Audrey and Daddy will be Horace."

Linda's language teacher was married to the head of the music conservatory and Linda had to audition for him. He assigned everyone to a music teacher, taking the most advanced himself.

In the midst of playing for him, Linda's mind went blank.

Dr. Marcum, who looked a lot like Winston Churchill, said, "That's all right, Old Dear." He must have seen potential because he took her for his own student.

Linda took ballet, enrolled for a classical record club, and subscribed to a news magazine. Her life had never been so broad. She was president of a campus club and had her own piano recital. She applied to work at Henry Street Settlement House in New York City during the summer following her second year, when she would graduate from junior college. Several teachers wrote recommendations that said she was intelligent, honest and reliable, including the Marcums.

It was the only time in her life that her father wrote her a letter. *"Dear Linda, I want you to know how dangerous New York City is..."*

She came home to Kansas City for spring break and was one of twelve finalists for the Miss Kansas City contest. She was pretty sure she would win; her plan was to go on to the state and national contests. Somehow she would work Henry Street Settlement House into her plans. She played the piano well during rehearsal.

The man who coached the contestants asked her, "I think you have a very good chance. Can you look at the audience and smile while you play?" Linda knew the Grieg Sonata did not allow for that.

Jean and Jim Jeff came to the contest but her parents didn't. Linda didn't win, didn't even come in second. She was stunned.

When she returned to school one of her friends asked her, "Well, you didn't expect to win, did you?"

But that was exactly what she expected. For the first time in her life, she had trouble studying and didn't do well on senior year final exams. When graduation day arrived and the graduate's names were called out, some followed by "With Honors," Linda wanted those honors but was afraid she had lost them in these last few weeks. Her name was called, "Linda Jones...," then there was silence and then, for the first time in the graduating class, "with Highest Honors."

Linda noted that while the graduation ceremony was going on, her parents were moving her belongings out of the dormitory. Freddy's parents, who had attended college themselves, were sitting in the graduation audience. Sometimes Linda thought to herself that other people appreciated her more than her parents.

When Linda joined her parents after the ceremony and told them she had graduated with highest honors, her mother asked, "What does that mean?" Linda felt like it was hopeless to try and explain, so she didn't.

"It's time now for you to learn to do something besides go to school all of the time," her father said later.

She hadn't the slightest idea what to do now that she was not going to be Miss Missouri or work with poor children in New York City. She wrote the people in New York and said, "I am not coming to the Henry Street Settlement House, you aren't going to give me enough money." She knew money wasn't really what she wanted; she had known all along the pay for the summer was $125. She felt like hurting herself more. Everything felt to her like "What's the use?"

That summer Mrs. Marcum called her and asked, "Now that you have graduated from our school, what will you be doing?"

The closest that Linda could come to an answer was to say that she was reading a biography of Wyatt Earp. She could feel her teacher's disappointment coming over the phone line.

Her parents, Jean and Jim Jeff all urged her to get a job. But when she looked in the newspapers, none of the employment ads seemed like anything she could or wanted to do.

The column under "Females" wasn't as long as the "Males" choices. Most under "Females" were listed as "Secretary," which not only didn't sound interesting, Linda wasn't even sure she had the needed typing skills. She was absolutely adrift.

And then she decided that the thing to do was get married.

"I am going to get married next year," she told Freddy. It was as if he could have first choice at the opportunity or step aside and let someone else apply for the position.

At first Freddy said, "I have to finish college and my Army obligation and get established." But Linda's tears and anger convinced him that he did not have time to do all that and then marry her.

In New York, Betty Friedan was writing a book, *The Feminine Mystique*, which stated that by the end of the nineteen-fifties, the average marriage age of women in America was 20 years of age; by that criteria Linda was already late. Next year she would be 21.

Meanwhile, Linda had to find a way to spend the year before the wedding. What gave her an idea was her parents saying that, "We certainly hope you never become a stewardess; it's so dangerous." Kansas City was the headquarters of TWA.

So she interviewed for a stewardess position and was chosen. She went through several weeks of training, memorizing the emergency exits and procedures for two engine Martins and four engine Constellations.

While Linda was flying she saw some of the eastern cities that she had never seen on the family trips out west: Washington, D.C., Boston, Miami. But it all felt slightly unreal. Linda didn't know who she really was, so she made up interesting people to be. At various times, she told her fellow crewmates, "I am Catholic," "I'm a farm girl;" all of it seemed more interesting than anything she actually knew about herself. She met an old boyfriend and dated him in

Baltimore. She was strongly attracted to him but he seemed part of this unreal world she was visiting before her real world started. The night before her wedding to Freddy she had flown on her last flight to Baltimore. She wanted to call Alan, badly, but she didn't.

Linda and Freddy were married in a lovely church service and received silver, china, crystal, towels, and sheets from their families and parents' friends. Marie and three other friends were Linda's bridesmaids.

Mrs. Wolff and Miss Lee, who had waited on Mrs. Jones and Linda at Harzfeld's all of those years, each sent lovely gifts.

Freddy's grandmother, when she saw Linda's family home, expressed her surprise. "Oh, I thought Linda's family was poor." On Linda's visits to Freddy's home town, Linda had offered to clean house for Freddy's grandmother.

Freddy and Linda didn't go on a honeymoon because Freddy felt they couldn't afford it. In fact she went home to her parents and he, to his, for the few weeks between the wedding and when school started again. He would begin graduate school and she would finish her third year of college now that she was a married woman.

They did have a weekend at a local motel. After the wedding Freddy was tired; his mother had given him some nerve pills. Linda was angry when he wanted to go straight to sleep. She had looked forward to finding out more about sex. "You must not love me if you don't want to make love to me," she said furiously.

So Freddy did what she insisted on, again, making love instead of going to sleep but immediately she realized that it hadn't been worth her effort. "Thank goodness I can at least have babies this way," she said to herself as she was falling asleep.

Chapter Five

The problem was that Freddy wanted to wait to have babies until he had finished school and the military service, and gotten a job. He told her, "At about age 35, I would like one child."

That was not what Linda had in mind at all and, to be fair, before they were married she had told him that she wanted five or seven children.

They sat down and had a discussion, after he told her what was in his mind and she didn't tell him what was in hers, they didn't discuss how they were going to go about not having babies.

November, 1959

Dear Marie,

I'm pregnant! My baby is due in the early summer. I don't mind so much that I throw up every morning. I just stamp my foot when I do. I take notes while I half-sleep through American Government class. I can't stand to walk into the supermarket because it smells but I have to. Oh well. I am getting what I want, but I feel a little guilty.

Your wedding was lovely. How are you and John doing? When are you all coming to Kansas City for Christmas? I can't wait to see you.

Love,
Linda

At last she knew who she was; she was a mother. Freddy

said, in a not very nice way, "That's the first thing you tell everyone, that you are going to have a baby." And, since he was right, it made Linda so angry that she slept on the floor all night, so she could punish Freddy. Linda was so anxious to tell the world that at last she knew who she was, that she put on maternity clothes long before she needed to.

At the end of the 1960 school year, Freddy went into the Army for six months; "Christmas help," they called it. Freddy and Linda packed the little '39 Chevy convertible, which Freddy had named "Benjamin, son of my sorrows," with a crib and blankets, towels and lamps, baby clothes from Tommy and the girls and, finally, there was only room left for Freddy to drive and Linda to sit in back, directly behind him.

At one point in the trip, all of their bedding fell out of the trunk and they backed up for a quarter mile along the shoulder of the highway until they had rescued everything.

They didn't call their parents when they arrived at Fort Sill, so Freddy's parents called the commanding officer. It would have been a terrible start to an army career that lasted longer than six months.

Soon after their arrival all of the new second lieutenants' wives were invited by the CO's wife to tea and Linda put on her best, biggest dress.

"When is your baby due?" Mrs. Barnes asked.

"In about three weeks," Linda answered.

"Have you been in to see the Army doctors yet?" Mrs. Barnes asked. When she heard that Linda had been told it would be a three week wait, she was outraged! "I want you to call me right away if you go into labor."

But there was time to go to the Army hospital and be sent to a town doctor because the Army hospital was full. Linda had been reading Grantley Dick Read's book, written during World War II, on painless labor and delivery, so she considered herself something of an authority and wanted to try and deliver her baby awake. There was something magical about this process.

"I've never seen a woman who could do it while she was awake and in the delivery room, I am the boss!" the town doctor declared firmly and finally.

Linda went home in tears and was so upset that Freddy came in the next week to talk to the doctor. Linda had confided to Freddy that she wanted him to be with her when the baby came but he had felt that he didn't want that, "I don't think I could make love to you again if I saw you like that."

They made plans for the July 4th weekend, so of course early on Saturday morning, Linda awoke, feeling like she had to go to the bathroom. But the feeling could not be satisfied and her back began to hurt also and she thought, "This might be labor."

"Wake up, Freddy." After Freddy was dressed, Linda carried her pillow for comfort and climbed into Benjamin the car. Freddy brought her ready overnight case and off they went to the hospital. The town doctor checked her and said, "This baby won't arrive before afternoon and I am going to the office."

They left Linda on the delivery table to go through labor with a young student nurse in attendance. In only a couple of hours, Linda felt the feeling that Jean had told her about, the bearing down feeling. The nurse said, "Oh no, don't push; the doctor isn't here," and hurried off to call him.

The doctor came in, introducing her to his brother, the anesthetist, as they brushed past her head. In a moment of levity brought on by the realization that this all would be over soon, Linda announced, "I've changed my mind; I'm not having a baby." But, from outside the room, all Freddy heard was Linda screaming, "No!"

Linda could hear them saying "She's crowning," just as they put her under. So, in the end when the baby arrived, no one was there but the doctors, the nurses and the baby.

"Your wife just had a lovely baby girl," the nurse announced to Freddy as she bustled out of the delivery room and on to other important things.

"My wife takes care of things like that," answered Freddy, as he sat with *The Longest Day* in his lap.

When Linda saw her baby girl the next day, she felt it was the happiest day of her life.

Chapter Six

It was hard to understand, then, why she wondered to herself, "Is this all there is to life?" as she carried the laundry basket into the house and sat in a chair folding clothes. She cared for her baby and cleaned the succession of small apartments that they called home; it seemed so endless. Freddy was finishing his active Army obligation.

Freddy was going through airborne training at Fort Benning in Georgia during the first presidential election when they both were old enough to vote. Airborne training was exhausting and Freddy had to get up at 4 a.m. every day.

He said to Linda, "I want you to go to bed early with me so I can get to sleep; you'll have to get up early too."

She made him breakfast and helped him break into his heavily starched fatigues and gave one final wipe to the spit-shined boots. When he left, Linda said to herself, "I'll sort of lay back down on the bed for a couple of hours until Marcella wakes up." Then she had trouble going to sleep with Freddy at 7 p.m..

They stayed up, however, to listen to the 1960 presidential candidates' first-ever televised debates. "I really like John F. Kennedy," Linda said to Freddy after the first debate. But she remembered all of the times her father had stormed around the house cursing, "The goddamned Democrats are going to give away the country." Jerry Jones had called Harry Truman absolutely every name in the book, although her mother, as a young woman, had been a precinct worker for him.

Actually Linda's parents had come to Kansas City as

Democrats, having come from southern-leaning families in a fence riding state. After someone told them that the Democrats were the Kansas City machine party, they switched to Republican and stayed with that party for the rest of their lives.

Freddy's parents, on the other hand, were Democrats but had a strong reservation about voting for Kennedy because "of the danger of the Pope dictating to the President of the United States" that their preacher had warned them about. Linda tried to talk them out of their fears, so much so that they thought she was voting for Kennedy but her father's words echoed so loudly in her head that she voted for Richard Nixon.

Freddy voted for Kennedy and they canceled each other out.

◆ ◆ ◆

One November evening after the elections, while doing dishes, Linda heard on the radio how Masters and Johnson in St. Louis were studying sexual intercourse and she thought to herself, "how very strange." She tried to picture couples copulating while doctors in white coats with clipboards watched.

In December, they moved back to Missouri and lived with Freddy's parents, Harold and Lorraine, in the big, old hotel where Freddy had grown up, while Freddy finished his masters' thesis. The hotel, over a hundred years old, was constructed of bricks hand-made by slaves. His grandparents had operated it, before his parents took over when Freddy was a baby. His grandmother's hotel dining room had been recommended by Duncan Hines. But Freddy's mother hated the dining room because she had to work in it while she was growing up; so now they just served breakfast.

Harold and Lorraine were delighted to have them where they could watch them closely. Once, before Linda and Freddy moved in with Harold and Lorraine, Harold had said, "I wish I was a little mouse living in your wall and I could watch you." Freddy, an only child, had slept in his parents' bedroom until he was 15 years old.

There was a maid and therefore Linda had no housework responsibilities. Linda's days were made up of bathing and feeding and chattering to Marcella and a good helping of boredom. Grandmother Lorraine taught the baby little tricks. When her grandmother asked, "How big are you, Marcella?" Marcella would raise her fat little arms as high as she could, to the top of her head.

Linda thought she might be pregnant again and weaned Marcella when she was just five months old. Maybe another baby would keep her busy enough. At bedtime, she set the baby on the porcelain table in the hotel dining room and gave her a juice glass of milk. Marcella grasped the glass with both hands and tipped it up to her mouth, drinking it down. After Linda put Marcella up in the bedroom to go to sleep, some nights the baby cried. Linda said, "Marcella should cry it out; she has to learn to go to sleep." Linda sensed this was hard on Lorraine but felt quite sure of her decision. Lorraine bit her lip but didn't interfere.

Freddy would be gone all the daylight hours, climbing over rocks and fences while mapping the geologic features of this county quadrangle. Linda didn't exactly know what was missing from her life, but decided to take a college course by mail, in world geography. Then, while Marcella slept, she carefully filled in the maps with colored pencils.

One day did stand out from all the boring rest. She sat on a chrome chair in the hotel lobby with Marcella on her lap and watched, with fascination, while the Kennedy inauguration unfolded in the Washington, D.C. snow. She was glad he had won, even if she hadn't voted for him. The whole story was so fascinating: a handsome, self-assured young president, his beautiful wife, little children and the possibility of more.

Linda went to visit her parents in Kansas City for a change. It was briefly satisfying to hear Nancy Jones as she berated Harold and Louis for their spendthrift ways, "If I was that tight, I would light my cigarettes with a ten dollar bill."

Cleo, who still worked for Nancy Jones, grinned at Marcella and said, "Hey, baby."

Linda asked after Cleo's son and grandson. "They're pretty fine," Cleo answered as she scrubbed the kitchen floor on her hands and knees.

Once a week, after church, they went with Freddy's parents to the Blue Moon on the highway and had a steak dinner for $2.95. Linda resented Freddy's dad telling, "Dress up; you're a beautiful young woman."

Evenings they watched television: Andy Griffiths, Dick Van Dyke and Mary Tyler Moore while Harold played poker in the lobby with the traveling men who stayed at the hotel. The days always finished with Freddy, Linda and his parents all sitting in the upstairs kitchen. Lorraine set her hair and both of his parents had a nightcap.

One particular night, Freddy's father was talking about how he "couldn't, even though I would if I could, rent a hotel room to any Negroes. If I did, the traveling men would never come back." There had been a lot in the newspapers recently about blacks seeking service at lunch counters and other public accommodations.

Linda was trying to reason with him about it and said, "But, Harold, what if everyone changed? What if everyone let the blacks come?" In a burst of strong feeling that she was afraid she couldn't contain, when she thought that she wasn't convincing anyone, she got up to leave the room. The lightweight chrome chair where she was sitting accidentally fell over as she stood, but she was not willing to admit it was an accident. So she and her father-in-law, who believed she knocked it over on purpose, didn't speak for several days. Linda's finger with the wedding ring began to itch.

Finally she said to Freddy, although she didn't think she really meant it, "If you don't get me out of here, I am going to divorce you."

Chapter Seven

June, 1961

Dear Marie,
Here we are in Illinois and it's so dirty. Freddy finally got a
job as an engineer because there aren't any jobs for geologists.
He's building a bridge.

Every morning I have to sweep up dead roaches before I can
take Marcella out of her crib. Our house is divided into two apart-
ments and I met the girl who lives in the back. She works in a
glove factory. She sat on the steps and smoked while her baby was
crying inside. I looked in and the baby was standing in a dirty lit-
tle dress in the corner of a crib and holding a bottle with what
looked like sour milk. Ugh.

I'm pregnant again; are you?

Love,
Linda

Marie had married her high school sweetheart and had a
baby boy about the same time that Linda had her girl but
Marie had also finished college and was teaching elementary
school; Marie's husband was going to the university for his
doctorate. Linda often had hurt feelings when Marie didn't
have much time to write back.

At the new job, Freddy became friends with another engineer, George, and when the two of them went dove hunting
on their off time, their wives, for lack of something else to
do, went shopping. George and Gladys were a little older
than Linda and Freddy and didn't have children so they

enjoyed Marcella. Marcella took her first steps at their small apartment on the birthday she turned one.

Even though her own father had always hunted and fished, it didn't seem to Linda that hunting was something Freddy would want to do. Shortly after their wedding Freddy had taken her up in the fire tower near his home. He reverentially showed her the sunset, offering it as a gift. She viewed it noncommittally and failed Freddy's test. He didn't say so but it was apparent to her. She wondered to herself why she couldn't measure up in the sensitivity department.

But then later she would wonder to herself, "Why would someone who appreciated sunsets so much want to shoot doves?"

◆ ◆ ◆

Meanwhile Linda surprised Freddy rather unpleasantly when she began studying Catholicism. The priest used an old fashioned catechism to teach her. She had already convinced herself years before that she was supposed to be a Catholic so she ignored most of the simple-minded platitudes that the priest used in his lessons. Linda started to attend mass at the parish church. It felt terribly rash to slip out very early every Sunday morning. Later she usually went to the Methodist Church with Freddy.

"Catholics the ones what eat fish?" her neighbor who lived in the back of her house asked, when Linda told her that she was a Catholic.

"On Fridays," Linda answered. She didn't add the part where she made two main dishes now every Friday, one for her, one for Freddy.

Shortly after that, those people moved out of the back of the house and Linda helped her landlady clean; she had never seen a home with rancid food covering the table and dirty diapers dropped all over the floor. Linda and Freddy decided to buy a new trailer because it would be cleaner than any house that was trapped in this town and Freddy liked the price. They picked one with two bedrooms, blue shutters and a flower box across the front. Linda planted portulaca in the flower box because the man at the hardware store said they didn't need much room for their roots and the flower box was really only a piece of guttering.

Then they were in the midst of moving to Virginia for another engineering job. They said goodbye and lost track of George and Gladys, like they had forgotten numbers of friends from their Army days. Linda was delighted to be pregnant again. She didn't want Marcella to get the feeling she was an only child, the curse she remembered so well from her own childhood.

They went to Missouri for a Christmas visit between life in Illinois and the move to Virginia. Their trailer was moved east by a company that moved house trailers.

They were visiting with Linda's parents in Kansas City when Linda woke up in the night, went to the bathroom and didn't make it back to bed. By morning she called Jean's doctor, "It feels sort of like labor but the baby isn't due for almost two months. Something must be wrong."

Freddy said, "I have to go to work." The headquarters of the engineering firm which hired him was in Kansas City and they were getting his report from the Illinois job and preparing to send him on to the job in Virginia.

Her father said "You just have the flu."

But her mother said, "Jerry, take this child to the hospital," after the paregoric that Jean's doctor prescribed didn't stop the pains. Her father didn't believe that she was really in labor so he dropped her off and let her carry her overnight case into the hospital herself.

This time they let her stay awake for the delivery and she was glad. Linda felt like she was really getting off easy: she hadn't gotten fat, didn't have to wait those last slow weeks and labor was not hard. They folded up the hospital bed like a recliner, much better than labor the first time on a flat, metal table. They gave her an anesthetic that deadened the bottom half of her body. As they moved her to the delivery table, she briefly wondered who those fat legs belonged to.

Just before the baby was born, Jean's doctor said, "Now let's hope this is a little girl; they have a better time of it when they're premature."

A few minutes later, after the baby just slipped out, they told her he was a boy and allowed her a glimpse before they wheeled him off in the Isolette.

Linda and Freddy, however, were sure everything would be fine. Freddy came to see her that night and they made plans; Freddy would go on to Virginia. Linda and the babies would stay with her parents until everyone was strong enough to fly east.

The next day Linda filled out all of the details on the birth announcements that Freddy had brought her. Freddy drove across the state singing "Unto Us a Son is Born." That evening her father and sister came to the hospital to visit since Freddy was gone. They came back from the nursery window looking worried but Linda assured them everything was fine.

In the night, the doctor woke Linda to try and explain something about the baby's breathing. He explained how a greasy coating was covering the baby's lungs. What he was saying was not very clear to her, so Linda tried to help him, "You mean that the baby only has a 50-50 chance?"

"Not nearly that good." And then the nurse came in to give her some medicine to put her to sleep.

In the morning she walked down the hall to look through the nursery window. There seemed to be a lot of activity; finally she was able to get someone to tell her the baby was dying. She asked, "Please call a priest." Linda stood her ground in the hall. When they told her the baby had died, Linda heard someone scream. Afterwards, she realized it was herself. They only allowed her into the nursery to touch the baby after he was dead. Linda reached tentatively into the Isolette and gently touched him with three fingers. He had black hair like Marcella had had.

The priest who arrived was a monsignor from a nearby church. An older Irishman with a warm smile, he looked like he had stepped from a movie about a kind old cleric, with Bing Crosby and a church named Saint Something or another, very much more personable than the Illinois pastor who had started her instructions. The monsignor came back to Linda's room after he had finished with final rites for the baby. Smiling at the distraught young mother, he posed her a riddle, "What's the worth of half a dime?"

Confused but momentarily distracted by his efforts and friendly old face, she learned that he was Monsignor Nichol and that he had just told a church full of little school children that he was going to bless a little angel. When he left, Linda sank easily into sleep.

The next day, when Linda returned from the hospital, her mother had dressed Marcella up in a blue gingham dress with a pinafore. Linda gathered Marcella into her arms and sat and rocked.

Chapter Eight

When they arrived in Virginia, they found a choral society that was delighted to get Freddy and would take Linda without audition to sing with the altos. Freddy had told his mother while they were dating, "Linda can play the piano."

His mother said "Oh good, she can accompany you."

Freddy had a strong baritone that he used from time to time in church choirs; sometimes he earned money as a soloist. Freddy also enjoyed theater and they began to read plays with two local groups. Freddy's interests provided them entree into some fine homes of the hunt country and once they even sang with the choral society in a lovely chapel in Upperville. The chapel was a donation from the Mellon family. They managed, mostly, to avoid mentioning that they lived in a trailer court, with a piano in their tiny living room.

Linda continued her study of Catholicism with the same parish priest who tended the John F. Kennedys in Upperville. He was ahead of the Pope in modernizing his church, using English and singing as part of his masses. Freddy's parents were pretty upset and Linda's father asked her, "Why would you do this to your marriage?" Linda didn't have any answer. She knew she was drawn by the mystery and ritual of the Catholic church. It was to her an "alone" religion that seemed to allow her to be herself, in church at least. Protestants were so friendly and human. They swallowed you up. But she couldn't and didn't put any of this into words; she just doggedly persevered in getting up early each

Sunday and attending mass, sometimes with Marcella in tow. Linda quietly, almost secretly observed her Catholic practices, another reason to feel guilty.

March, 1962

Dear Marie,

I am going to ask your mother to be my sponsor in the Church. Do you think she will say yes?

At last I have a friend in the trailer court here in Virginia. Her name is Barbara. Her husband is an engineer like Freddy and they also decided to live in a trailer since they are always moving. They are a little older than us and have three kids. The whole family is into scouting.

Now I don't feel quite so lonesome.

Freddy and I are singing (yes, they really let me and I do try hard.) We do Bach and Handel. And we are reading plays with two different groups. Barbara's oldest daughter babysits for us so I can go too. I think I really am a high-brow and didn't know it.

Barbara is such a good person; she reminds me of you. I like to just be around her. When I told Mama Barbara's way of waking her children in the morning is to kiss them, Mama said it is strange. But I don't think it is strange. I am determined to get pregnant again as soon as I can. I don't want to stay in this sad place and grieve for my baby. I want to have another one and forget.

Love,
Linda

Within a couple of months, Linda was pregnant again. Jean discovered that she was pregnant also, at 39. "This is definitely not in our plans," she told her sister, "and I'm due just a couple of months after you. I'm sorry; it's not fair of me to take some of the attention away from you."

Linda was puzzled by Jean's feeling because she was delighted to share this experience of womanhood with her sister. Linda always wanted to be a peer with Jean but never quite felt like she'd succeeded.

The sisters shared their pregnancies long distance. Jean was worried that she was so old that she would never get her figure back.

With evenings of adult stimulation to look forward to, Linda could enjoy relaxing in the sun, reading to Marcella at naptime, smelling the apples when fall came.

Just a little earlier in the pregnancy than last time, about two months too soon, one day as she was doing her housework, Linda's abdomen felt very heavy. She fretted about whether to call the doctor, then she called the doctor and made an appointment and, after Freddy came home from work, fumed at herself as Freddy drove them to town, "I'm just being ridiculous."

But she wasn't ridiculous; "You are five centimeters dilated, half-way to delivering the baby," the doctor said. The doctor put on a brave face for her but sent her immediately to the hospital. On the way there, Linda asked Freddy, "If this baby dies, can we take him back to Kansas City and bury him beside Sean?"

A young resident at the hospital suggested to Linda's doctor, "Why not try the new procedure?" They could put stitches around her cervix to hold in the baby.

Linda's doctor thought it all pretty hopeless but had no answer to the resident's question, "What can we lose?"

So they performed the procedure, sedated her to keep her quiet, and elevated the foot of the bed to keep her upside down, more or less. Linda could hear on a radio in the ward that Eleanor Roosevelt was dying; it was November 7, 1962. Linda called her parents "It's sokay; I'm awright..." but they couldn't understand what she was saying.

The baby stayed put in utero for a week, two weeks, a month and was safe. They were going to spend Christmas Day with Barbara and her husband and children. Linda asked Freddy, "Will you put Marcella in her snowsuit?" Freddy was busy fiddling with the dials on the new combination hi-fi phonograph/radio and didn't hear her. He had decided that he needed a new toy to keep him happy if they were going to be shut in this winter with another baby. A little annoyed, Linda grabbed the wiggly two-year-old and stuffed her into the suit. "You get the cake and fruit salad," she said as she headed out the trailer door. This time he heard her.

Linda and Marcella held hands and skipped through the snow, saying, "Hippity hop to the barber shop to get a stick of candy, one for you and one for me and one for baby brother."

Linda had told Marcella for a total of two years now, "You are going to have a baby brother," even though there was really no way to know. She had felt this was the case.

The two families had a lovely holiday celebration.

The next day they left little Marcella with Barbara while they went to have the baby delivered. The doctors would cut the stitches out and give Linda pitocin to start labor. It was the newest thing: babies by appointment.

When the baby finally arrived and Freddy saw him in the nursery, shortly after delivery, he came back to Linda and said, "He's my favorite color, red." Linda had made a careful study and found George Washington University Hospital was one of the few hospitals which allowed the babies to room in with the mothers, at least during the day. When he was finally brought to her, after circumcision, he lay whimpering in her arms but she felt very glad to hold him. Linda held him as much as she could for the five days in the hospital.

When Linda asked the pediatrician in the hospital how often she should feed the baby, she said, "Whenever he's hungry."

"That's good, because that's what I would have done anyway."

Marcella's doctor has said, two years before in the dark

ages of Oklahoma, "I don't want you to feed this baby but every four hours," so Linda felt a little guilty nursing her every two hours when she cried.

Freddy asked Linda, "Why do you pay to go to doctors if you don't do what they say?"

Freddy brought Marcella to the hospital with him to pick up Linda and the new baby. He left her with a grey lady in the lobby since she wasn't allowed to come upstairs. Just as Linda, Freddy, and a nurse carrying the baby came down in the elevator, Marcella appeared around the corner with her grey lady in tow and announced, "Oh, there's my baby brother!"

Chapter Nine

Marcella cried out when she awoke in the night to see Mommy rocking Andy and nursing him; that was too much of a shock. She would have to share her mother with her baby brother. Mommy had to rock Andy a lot. He was almost always crying.

Freddy said to Linda, "You never pay any attention to Marcella and me. You're always rocking the baby."

"Well, maybe that'll improve," Linda answered, "I found out that I can lay him, tummy down, over a hot water bottle and he'll quiet down for a while. While he's quiet, I am going to box up my maternity clothes and send them to Jean."

Freddy pointed out, "Jean is gonna' have her baby in a couple of months; why waste the postage?" Linda couldn't think of a reasonable answer but she wanted to share with Jean in every way she could.

Linda, Freddy and the children drove to Kansas City six weeks after Andy was born to have him christened by Monsignor Nichol, who had baptized Sean, and because Linda wanted to be in Kansas City when Jean had her baby. After a long weekend Freddy drove back while Linda and the children stayed with Nancy and Jerry and they all waited for the other baby, who seemed to be taking his or her own time.

While Linda was taking a bath one night, Andy started to cry. Nancy went into the bedroom and discovered that Linda had placed him over a hot water bottle to buy herself a little free time. Nancy opened the bedroom window and threw the hot water bottle out, furious with Linda. She barged into the bathroom, "What are you thinking of? That baby's in pain!" Nancy insisted that Linda get out of the tub. She hurried matters along by giving Linda a little shove into the bedroom. Linda thought maybe her mother might be right, that she herself was not a good mother. She was always looking for easier ways to do things.

In early March, Jean finally delivered a little girl and named her Fiona. While Jean was in the hospital, Aunt Linda fed the three older children their breakfast every morning and got them off to school. Then she visited Jean in the hospital, carrying gifts for her or the baby, Russell Stover pastel mints, a silk bonnet, while her mother watched her own children. Finally she could delay no longer and Linda and the children flew home to Virginia. The first night back she begged Freddy, "Please let's just go out to eat. I'm too tired to cook."

Freddy, however, was nothing if he wasn't frugal. "Eating out isn't cheap," Freddy pointed out, and not something he liked to do, unless it was at someone else's expense. So Linda began dinner preparations in a fog. She decided, since they couldn't go to Johnson's Steak House, that hamburgers and french fries sounded good to her.

Linda put Andy into his feeding table and turned in the small trailer kitchen to fill a pan on the stove with grease. Andy began to fuss and her attention was diverted. Linda didn't notice immediately that the fat was getting too hot. When it began to smoke, she rushed over and cut off the fire, abandoning her plans to french fry as too ambitious. "I remember that hot liquids can break glass..." she thought to herself, as she poured just a little back into the jar. Everything seemed fine, so she poured the rest of the hot grease in and then watched as the jar began to marbleize in front of her eyes. Suddenly she realized that she had bare feet and that the trailer kitchen floor was very small and would suddenly be covered with hot grease. She turned to leave quickly, the pan with a little hot grease still in her hand, and ran into Marcella, spilling the remaining grease down the side of Marcella's head and arm. Marcella's shriek woke her up. Linda felt angry. "Marcella, you aren't supposed to be here!"

Then, as if someone had changed the slide in a projector and she could see another view, she thought, "I've just poured hot grease down the side of my child; she could die." Linda flung the pan wildly, fortunately missing Andy, grabbed up her daughter and ran to the bathroom, yelling "Freddy, Freddy!"

Freddy was reading a book. He finally heard his wife yelling, "Call the doctor...we have to go to the hospital... help, Freddy, help me," as she fought Marcella to hold her head under the bathtub faucet.

Since recent articles in newspapers and magazines had recommended cold water for burns, Linda was trying to get Marcella's head under the running water. Marcella didn't want her head held under the water and fought, but did allow her mother to get her arm under the faucet. When Freddy finally understood the seriousness of the situation, he picked up the baby and they headed to Barbara's to drop him off and go to the hospital. The trip was like a long, bad nightmare, complete with wrong turns and an elusive goal but, at last, they were there.

The tall, lanky town doctor was reassuring as he said "The arm is probably much worse than the face. The tricky thing about burns is how they don't look awful right away." The doctor coated the burns and they came home with some medicine.

October, 1963

Dear Marie,

My little girl had a perfect little face and I have hurt it. It makes me feel so sad. I pray it won't stay but right now it is awful.

People stare at us and some of them point and make comments. She has lost her hair on one side of her head. The plastic surgery doctor at Johns Hopkins said he cannot operate until later.

Please let me know what is going on in your life. I think it is neat that we each have one boy and one girl. Are you going to Kansas City for Christmas?

Love,
Linda

What Linda didn't tell Marie was that she had a way of expecting Marcella to be older for her age and, oddly enough, Marcella was. It almost seemed as if she was born a very old soul who bore everything in great dignity but she was also a three year old baby.

◆ ◆ ◆

That fall President Kennedy was shot and killed on Jerry Jones' birthday. He had always said, "The goddamned Kennedys think they are better than everyone else." But on November 22, 1963, he was pretty thoughtful.

Chapter Ten

Thanks to Freddy's interest in theater and Linda's search for something more in her life. she tried out for, danced, and sang in the chorus of "Oklahoma!" with the local drama group when she was a few weeks pregnant again. This, in spite of the warning given by the ladies in Freddy's hometown who felt compelled after she lost her second baby, that she "mustn't be so active when pregnant." The pregnancy didn't show. Unlike when she was wearing maternity clothes unnecessarily to show the world that she was pregnant the first time, now she wanted to show the world that she could have children and do other things too. So, as the pregnancy progressed, she would lie down on the bed with her abdomen flat, and slip on a lightweight girdle from the dimestore. No one guessed she was expecting. Linda didn't even want to talk about being pregnant. She was pleased but now she was going to be something more than just a wife and mother. Actually she never considered herself a housewife. "I never married a house," she would say to herself.

After a taste of the stage in "Oklahoma!", she tried out for a part in Moss Hart's "You Can't Take it with You." At first she had a supporting part, but when the young woman who was Alice kept missing rehearsal, they chose Linda to play Alice. It was a romantic part and it was heavenly to feel young, carefree and attractive. She developed a crush on the young man playing opposite her. Her feeling was reciprocated and she felt a little guilty. After the last performance, everyone went to a cast party but she told them she couldn't, "My keeper won't let me," but really it was her own conscience.

◆ ◆ ◆

Linda was asked to substitute teach French and Spanish classes at the high school for three weeks while Barbara watched the children for her. Linda doubted if she was really qualified but the sleepy school system wasn't terribly demanding. Two of the students in her French class had come from the all black high school, chosen for their academic abilities to begin the process of integration. Linda felt particularly in over her head in the French class. She was supposed to be temporary but the man who had hired her didn't seem to be searching for a replacement. When a candidate finally showed up to monitor the classes, Linda told Barbara, "I fear my own inadequacies are very obvious."

Then Barbara said, "We just heard that we will be moving soon," and Linda's short career had to come to an end. The day that Barbara's family moved, their younger daughter sat rocking Andy in the little trailer living room, their soft blond heads together; the little girl's tears falling on the baby's head.

After they pulled out, Linda hid in the back of her trailer and sobbed. She felt so lonely losing her good friend. But it wasn't long before Linda and Freddy sold the trailer and moved also, to a house across the river in Maryland. As soon as the one engineering job was finished, it was time to go on to the next.

It was there in their house on River Road that they met the Hanrahans.

Linda was bathing the children one night after baby Heather was born when the sirens of several fire trucks excited them so much that Linda held the naked children, wrapped in towels, up to the window so they could watch as the trucks stopped just down the street. Freddy took off in that direction. He came back after a bit to announce, "The Hanrahans just rented that old frame house down the road, the one that has been vacant. They turned on the heat and didn't know there wasn't any water in the boiler. They nearly set the house on fire!"

Freddy filled buckets and pitchers with water to carry to the Hanrahans because now all of their water was off and he announced, "I invited them for dinner and a shower tomorrow night." Freddy coined a name for their new neighbors: the Great, Unwashed Hanrahans.

Linda liked them immediately when they piled in the back door the next night.

David was like a big bear of a man. Smiling, he ushered the two children up the stairs to the bathroom.

Long earrings flashing, Adriane filled Linda in on the previous evening's adventure. Watching the earrings, Linda remembered how she had believed until now, this minute, that pierced ears and long earrings were tacky.

After their bath, Marcella took Holly, the little girl, off to color with crayons.

"What happened to your face?" Holly asked Marcella.

"That's my sore face; I got burned," Marcella said as she pushed up the head band her grandmother had made her. Nancy had sewn a number of wide velvet ribbons in pastel colors with elastic and mailed them to Marcella to partially cover the burn until her operations could begin the next year. The doctors were going to slowly excise the scar tissue over several operations because as they explained to Freddy and Linda, "The scalp is elastic and we can restore her hairline."

Andy and little David discovered they had similar interests as they rolled small trucks across the floor; they were also of an age.

Adriane Hanrahan said, "People think we are hippies."

Linda asked, "What is a hippy?"

"Oh, they have long hair, smoke dope, protest the war, dress different."

Far as Linda could see, the Hanrahans fit the bill.

After dessert, Adriane suggested, "Let's take turns swapping children so we each have free days." This was a new idea. Linda had brought home other children for her kids but she hadn't the foggiest notion what she would do with a free day of her own. She finally settled on leaving Andy and little Heather with Adriane so that she could take Marcella for swimming lessons. It was problematic for Linda to be without any of her children; she thought people would not then be able to tell who she was. Freddy remained concerned about living frugally so they didn't hire sitters and go out together much without the children. Being with Freddy, being a wife, didn't serve the same need for identification that being with her children did anyway.

Adriane was really very brave to take Heather, who transformed from being a perfect little third baby to a toddler that could and did get into everything. In Adriane's non-baby proof house with paints and other crafts materials, Heather could set the world on its ear. Adriane's life was filled with art, not just dishes and dusting and washing. She made crafts and sold them to stores in Georgetown. Linda said, "I've never even been to Georgetown."

So they made plans for child care and went. In and out of the little stores, some on back alleys, Linda picked up items, "What's this?"

And Adriane seemed to know the answers, "That's a french cheese grater. See, you turn the handle like this."

It was a wonderful afternoon of discovery. Linda remembered every detail for years.

David was a sculptor and turned the shed behind their rented house into a studio. He was applying to become a Rhodes scholar. They were going to go to Greece to live for a year.

Linda kept remarking, "Holly looks like big David, but who does little David look like?"

She asked the question more than once until finally Adriane told her, "Neither of the children are big David's. I was married to another man and I left him and came to live with David just before we moved in across River Road."

This shocked Linda. David was so solicitous of the children, such a good parent. A little voice in her head whispered, "Adriane might be an agent of the devil sent to introduce you to things better stayed away from," but Linda also felt Adriane was the single most fascinating person that she had ever met. Adriane felt Linda was calm, serene and together and she found it interesting that Linda believed in an anthropomorphic god.

Linda went to look up *anthropomorphic* in the dictionary.

The Hanrahans were saving their money for a trip to Greece. Most people would have felt they couldn't have lived on as little money as the Hanrahans had coming in, let alone saved any for a dream. The strain showed from time to time, Adriane said, "Being poor is a challenge but sometimes you get tired of being challenged." She had called their landlord several times to get the boiler fixed and finally she had called his wife, crying. That worked.

She also told Linda about her brother's letters from Vietnam. Vietnam was a place that the evening news talked about in Linda's ear while she prepared dinner and fed the baby. Linda knew it was important to help the South Vietnamese save their country from Communism. But Adriane was saying, "That's not what's happening." And she told Linda awful things that her brother had told her. One story in particular stayed in Linda's mind. The soldiers set a rat on fire to watch it run. What Adriane said wasn't enough to change Linda's mind that the government knew best, but it was enough to put a little crack in her conviction.

One night, as Linda watched Andy playing, her eyes

filled with tears and she said to Freddy, "We could rear him and love him and someday he could be sent off to war and killed."

◆ ◆ ◆

That summer, Linda went with the children to Kansas City for a visit. Her mother said, "Your father has to have an operation but he asked Dr. Donlan to wait a couple of weeks so that he can visit with you and the children."

Linda and her dad went to Montgomery Wards and bought the parts to put up a swing set for the children. Jerry Jones was taking the parts out and fitting them together even as Linda said, "Wait, Daddy, I haven't read the directions." Linda wanted to put the set together with her father.

Jerry and Nancy assured both daughters that, if anything ever happened to their father, "You will each inherit a substantial amount of money." The two week visit went by and just a few days before Linda and the children were due to leave, Jerry was operated on.

Linda sat with her mother and sister in the waiting room until Doctor Donlan came out and said, "Everything went well and it looks like we got it all out." He had delivered Linda almost thirty years before and was still practicing. Jerry wanted to have his friend take care of him.

Linda returned to Maryland in time for Marcella to start kindergarten and gave it little more thought. Her father was hurt that she didn't ask after him when she called home but no one told her about the trip back to the operating room and the hemorrhages. Her mother seemed to be saying that her father was doing well. It was pretty hard on Nancy who needed to drink a little more in order to stand it.

That Christmas, Linda and Freddy and the children flew back to Missouri to visit their families. Her father had gone back to work part time. Linda was in the kitchen with her mother when she said, "I hear the garage door going up;

Daddy must be coming home." Linda opened the basement door to greet him.

There was an old man coming up the basement stairs. It was all she could do to keep from screaming. Her father, who had always been a handsome man, had aged 30 years in the three months since she last saw him and no one had realized it or thought to warn her.

Chapter Eleven

Freddy kept telling Linda that he had met another young couple that had a boy the age of Andy and a girl the age of Heather and he wanted her to meet them. Finally she met the Lindstroms and they impressed her also. Eric was tall and large; Jeannie was poised and gentle; both were attractive. They seemed so sure of themselves. Unlike the Hanrahans, they were mainstream but not uptight. Once, Linda and Freddy went with the Lindstroms to a party in Potomac. An elderly gentleman who was a guest at the party remarked, after meeting the two couples, "I don't fear for the future of the country when I meet such fine young people."

It gave Linda great pride to introduce the Lindstroms to the Hanrahans and the Hanrahans to the Lindstroms; she felt as if she and Freddy were more interesting people for having such friends. Linda and Jeannie began to trade their children back and forth; sometimes Andy spent two days with the Lindstroms' son and sometimes it was the other way around. This would be a big help when Marcella's operations began. The boys were well-suited to each other, being blond, deliberate fellows. They became fast friends. In a way, Andy had become Freddy's alter ego. Freddy, always witty, would make jokes about Andy's cautious approach to life. At first Linda did not see that the jokes were at Andy's expense.

And the two couples also put the baby girls, Heather and Zaza, together. They also seemed well-matched. Because Heather could climb, she would climb out of the playpen to fetch toys but, because Zaza was in the playpen, she would climb back in. As they grew, the little girls were constantly breathing down their brothers' necks.

February, 1966

Dear Marie,

How are you all? You must be pregnant because I am again! I'm frightened. Heather will be only 18 months old when this baby arrives. It's the same month that Marcella starts first grade. I am not at all sure I can do it. But you do it—and teach too. How on earth do you manage to also take care of three small children and also work?

Love,
Linda

Every time Linda had a baby, Marie had a baby within a few months, so that each of them presently had one boy and two girls. Marie wrote back that she wasn't pregnant and then, two weeks later, wrote back that she was.

◆ ◆ ◆

One night Jean called,"Daddy is having nosebleeds that won't stop. You might want to think about coming for a visit again."

Linda knew, she just knew but she also told herself that she didn't know. She flew to Kansas City with the children. When she arrived, they weren't sure what to tell Jerry. Nancy, Jean and Jim Jeff did not want to tell him that his cancer had returned. Linda thought they were wrong but, as the youngest, she figured she was probably wrong and kept her thoughts to herself.

When she told her mother that she was pregnant again, Nancy told Linda, "You mustn't tell your father; he would just worry." She also said, " We have discussed taking the children away from you because we didn't feel you could take care of them." Linda was stunned and feared there might be truth in what her mother said. She knew she was responsible for Marcella's burn. She wasn't as careful as her mother and sister. Freddy and Linda had agreed that, unlike their own parents who had always urged caution, they would encourage their children to take risks. She was unsure what was right.

Her mother had always kept Linda clean, with ribbons in her hair and polished shoes. She had always known where Linda was, had always prepared three meals a day with all of the required servings of vegetables and fruits. With three children, Linda had to compromise and sometimes she was so tired. On a pay phone away from the house, she cried to Freddy, "Jean and Jim Jeff say the children drive Mama crazy and Mama says Jean and Jim Jeff can't stand the children. I don't feel comfortable at either place." Still she stayed.

Linda told the children, "You have to pretend like you are grownups and not make lots of noise because Granddaddy is very sick."

It was hard for Jerry, who was bed-ridden and in pain, to understand why he didn't get better. "I just wonder if this will go on forever," he asked in exasperation.

Linda pointed out to him , "Daddy, however this ends, it will not go on forever." That seemed to be of some comfort.

They kept Jerry at home and Nancy busied herself with cleaning and ironing his pajamas and fixing his meals but she couldn't sit with him. There wasn't enough whiskey in the world to make that possible. They hired nurses to come night and day.

One night Linda carried Andy in to be kissed by his grandfather, "Goodnight, Ludwig." Jerry Jones nicknamed Andy after the Chancellor of West Germany because of his fat, round blond baby face. Linda knew her father worried about his family, about who would take care of them if something happened to him. He worried mostly about Jean and Jim Jeff's financial well-being. They always seemed to spend all they had and then some. The same couldn't be said about

Linda and Freddy. Their fathers joked "that Freddy would be a millionaire by the time he was 35 but still have his first nickel."

As time passed and it was near Easter, Jean and Jim Jeff decided that Dr. Donlan should be replaced, that he didn't know enough about the latest medical advances and they called in a younger man, one of their acquaintances. The new doctor believed Jerry should be told the truth. He told Jerry that he was suffering from terminal cancer.

After that conversation, Linda walked into her father's room. Daddy was gone, replaced by a stranger, a thin old man lying on the bed. He looked like someone from a third world country, barely alive. Her father lapsed into an unconscious state for days. Three weeks later, Linda had taken the late evening shift to relieve the nurse. Rain fell outside the black window, lulling her to sleep. When her head fell over and hit the back of the chair and bounced her awake, she reached over and felt that her father's pajamas were soaked. She went to get the nurse. "I think Daddy's pajamas should be changed."

After finishing the job, the nurse sought out Linda and Jean and asked them, "Do you want me to wake your father? He's in such a deep sleep; he may never awaken."

"No, there's no point in waking him up to be in pain," the daughters answered together.

He awoke from the stuporous sleep he had lain in on his own, sat up for the first time in days, and called out. When they came to his doorway, he said,"I was almost gone, wasn't I? Please call my brother to come over and bring your mother into the bedroom."

The rain continued to fall and when they all were sitting on or about his bed, Jerry patted his wife's hand and said, "Thank you for being a good wife and raising the girls as ladies." He turned to his brother, "You can have the outboard motors and please see that Mom is taken care of."

Their mother would outlive all of her sons. He said, "I expected life to be short, but not this short." Having been born just after the turn of the century, Jerry Jones was 64 years old.

Sometime in the middle of the night, Linda said, "Daddy, you should go to sleep, you'll get overtired."

He just looked at her because this time he knew that he would never talk to them again. After he fell back into sleep, his heart continued to beat for several days but they all felt that he left that Easter night after he talked with them.

April, 1966

Dear Marie,

My Daddy died right after Easter. I was in Kansas City for two months with the children during his final illness. I have his duck calls just because I wanted to have something that was his. Jean and Jim Jeff think there's another will. Daddy and Mama always said each of us would inherit a substantial amount of money but the only will we could find said that Daddy gave each of us ten dollars and the rest to Mama. Jean and Jim Jeff think there's some mistake; maybe the most recent will was lost. Mama still will live in the big house alone. J and J tried to talk her into moving to a senior community, where she wouldn't be so lonely. But she says this house is all she has.

I suggested she could ask Cleo to come live with her but she is afraid Cleo's friends would want to come visit and what would the neighbors say!

Love,
Linda

That spring a noisy redwing blackbird landed on Nancy's patio and fussed at her until she took it food. Every April after that, as long as she lived in the house, the redwing blackbird returned at the same time each year, just after the anniversary of her husband's death.

Chapter Twelve

The green and white tiles stretched out before Linda, who was on her hands and knees. She had arisen from a sick bed, mumps that she caught from the kids, to scrub the kitchen floor. The floor had bothered her with its insidious stickiness. Besides, she had already stayed in bed for three days. That should be enough.

When Linda finally started to pull her pregnant self up, she could not raise her head without the most excruciating pain. She took a couple of aspirin and tried to lie down but the pain seemed to be waiting there for her in a cloud on the bed. She wanted to raise her head up out of the pain but it followed her. She turned her head from side to side and the pain became steadily worse. By nightfall she was crazy and begging, "Freddy, please just kill me."

Nothing, no pain killers were making any difference. Freddy was on the phone with Linda's doctor, who was on the phone with the hospital, trying to get a room for Linda. But no hospital wanted her, not in their maternity ward with her viral infection.

Finally the doctor said to the hospital, "How would you like it if I blow this to *The Washington Post*: Hospital Refuses Pregnant Patient with Encephalitis?" So, at midnight, Adriane came over to stay with the children and Linda fell into the back of the station wagon so that Freddy could drive her to the hospital. Linda was vaguely aware when they arrived.

They loaded her on a gurney and rolled her upstairs and

into a private room with a bright light shining in her face and left her for what seemed like hours. They were trying to find a private nurse to take care of her; one that wouldn't be near their other pregnant patients. After the nurse came and the morphine shots began, Linda slept for most of eight days. She would awaken when a meal arrived and think, "I should really eat something." Then she would fall asleep until the next meal. The intravenous line kept Linda and the baby from starving.

Freddy came one evening to visit. Linda excused herself to go into the bathroom. She put her head down on the sink and fell asleep.

When she emerged, Freddy said, "Well, visiting hours are over. It's been a pleasure," and kissed her goodbye.

The night before she was to go home in the morning, she was able to watch an entire television show without falling asleep.

In Kansas City, Jean and Jim Jeff had planned for Nancy to come along on their trip to New Mexico and share the expenses. They needed her to come along to make their trip possible. Jim Jeff reasoned, "Your mom won't be able to go east to help Linda since there's an airline strike going on and no planes are flying." If they told her that Linda was very ill, she might not leave with them. So they didn't tell her until they were on the way.

"Nancy, Linda caught mumps from the kids and they think it's gone into encephalitis."

Nancy called Freddy that evening from the motel, she asked "Freddy, what does this mean? Will it affect her brain?"

Freddy answered, "Well, Nancy, how will we ever know?"

Nancy was not amused. Freddy was taking it all a little lighter now that the crisis seemed past.

Nancy never actually told Jean that she was angry at them for not telling her before they left, but she knew that Jean very much wanted a pair of beaded moccasins, so she bought a pair of full dress Oglala Sioux moccasins for Linda instead.

It was difficult for Freddy at home; he took time off to take care of the children. He had never changed diapers. He would undo the safety pins and ask, "Marcella, would you help your sister step out of her diaper?"

When Linda came home on a Saturday from the hospital, there were little piles of everything everywhere, the sort of thing that drove her crazy. It was a good thing that ladies from both the Catholic and Methodist churches brought meals because it totally exhausted Linda to just eat one-half a sandwich. Mostly she lay on the hammock in the yard and watched the children play.

She opened a card, *Dear Linda, Your mother told my mother that you had encephalitis/meningitis. I am so worried about you. Are you okay? I hope you get well soon. Love, Marie*

On Monday, Freddy went back to work. That evening Adriane came over to play a new Beatles album for Linda, who asked her, "Why are the Beatles singing, 'I get hives?'"

Linda was tired almost all of the time. Freddy felt like the encephalitis had changed her personality. One evening Linda asked Marcella, "Please keep an eye on Heather while I go upstairs to the bathroom."

As Linda was coming back downstairs, Freddy asked her, "Why is a strange man walking across the yard from River Road, carrying Heather?" Marcella's six-year-old attention had wandered and little Heather had headed straight for the busy street. They were very lucky that a driver spotted her through the dusk and stopped. Linda felt so guilty; it was one of the times she thought her mother was right. She was too careless to be a good mother.

Freddy came home from the library with a book for Linda titled *Most Of Us Are Mainly Mothers*. Linda wanted to throw it at him. While she was still pregnant, Freddy began to talk about buying a house but it was impossible for Linda to think about uprooting herself at this time. Freddy said, "I want a house on the edge of a park so it looks like it has more land or with a view of water, under $50,000." Real estate agents laughed at the idea.

In September baby Carroll arrived. She was tiny and pretty and perfect, a lot like a Betsy-wetsy baby doll. As she left the maternity ward, Linda had trouble believing this could be the last time for a long time that she would have a baby. She knew their budget and relationship and her body couldn't support more babies now, but she promised herself it wouldn't be forever. She was only 28. Having babies had been the most important part of her life.

When she got in the car, Andy said, "Mama, you can't have another boy, can you?"

"No, Andy, I guess not."

Nancy had come to take care of the other children. She said to Linda, "Oh, Honey, you look so, so..."

Linda finished the statement for her with "old."

Nancy drank too much every evening during her visit and then got up during the night, coming downstairs and doing strange things, like hiding the cookies that she had made during the day.

While her mother was still there, Linda went to the beauty shop and clothes shopping on her mom's money. At least this time, thanks to the encephalitis, she had her figure back, not that Freddy didn't caution her about not getting fat. When she was feeling down, Freddy would say "Chin up, now the other one."

Freddy asked her "Why do you go to the beauty shop and pay them lots of money, if you always come out crying?"

She decided he was right and this time when she went, she told the hair stylist, "Cut all of the old permanent off because I'm never coming back." 1966 was a good year to make the decision to grow your hair and leave it natural. The long hair would be just right with the long skirts and moccasins that were replacing the short dresses and tailored skirts and sweaters in her wardrobe.

It was hard for anyone else to take care of baby Carroll because she would not take anything from a bottle. When Linda returned from her beauty respite, her mother had spent hours walking with the baby.

Adriane made ratatouille and brought it over. She told Linda, "I like your mom; she doesn't take anything off anyone." Nancy Jones, although she also liked Adriane, did not approve of her kitchen. She had seen Adriane use unwashed mushrooms and so when Adriane was gone, Nancy poured the ratatouille down the drain and into the garbage.

Jeannie Lindstrom came and took Andy and Heather for a couple of days to help the burgeoning household. Adriane, who was concerned for her friend, asked Linda, "Have you read Betty Friedan's *The Feminine Mystique*? The U.S. is in danger of overtaking India's birthrate." Linda had trouble concentrating after the brain fever and didn't have much time to read.

In later years, Linda would keep track of the 60s by her pregnancies. While the rest of the world was making martyrs and mayhem, she had been making babies. Sometime after baby Carroll was born, Linda was reading a magazine in a doctor's office. She saw an article by Masters and Johnson that said, in a little blow-up box, "We ask women if they experience orgasm and if they say they don't know, we take that to be a negative answer."

Linda realized that was her.

Part Two

Chapter Thirteen

When the real estate agent called, she said, "I have two houses that fit Freddy's criteria for you to look at. One is right on the banks of the C & O Canal, with a view of the Potomac River but it is in an area that, although it's close to Washington D.C., seems almost carved out of West Virginia. You probably won't be interested in that one. The other house is in the District and sits on a cliff also overlooking the Potomac River. It's in a very good neighborhood."

The first house was locked and they couldn't get in, but when Linda saw the house and the setting adjacent to the canal she told Freddy, "This is it."

"But you haven't even seen the inside and, besides, we haven't looked at the other house!" Freddy argued.

"I don't care; this is it." Linda said, as she sat down on the stone steps. There was a vista of the canal and the river, opening up right off the backyard.

So they took gifts of money from their parents, three times more from her mother, and used the money to put a down payment on the house.

It was dangerously close to the river for a family with such young children, but the setting was so beautiful that, after they moved in, absolute strangers would knock on the door and ask them, "Please let us know if you are ever interested in selling," and they would leave their names and phone numbers.

Several of the rooms in the new house were painted brown and Linda could hardly stand that. She decided to paint the little girls' room a bright, light yellow herself. She knew that Freddy was worried about her doing the painting because she had never painted much and, as Andy said, "Mom, you and I have wobbly hands, don't we?"

But she decided to go ahead and try to be very careful. When she was through, she felt she had done a pretty good job, although there was one spot on the white ceiling with a little yellow paint. That evening she proudly showed Freddy the job, with a little apology for the spot on the ceiling.

"Didn't you put masking tape around the edge?" he asked.

"No," she answered.

Freddy was so angry that he doubled his fist and hit the door, leaving a dent where his blow landed. Linda felt that there was little she could do well, except have babies, and she even need extra help with that.

◆ ◆ ◆

Almost immediately the new community began to come to their doorstep; a neighbor invited them to join a pool that would be built if there were enough members to invest $450. Linda found herself going to town meetings. The town had a small newsletter; she avidly awaited its arrival each month to read it.

The school was small; the teachers' expectations of the children in the community were very modest. When Linda became involved in the tiny PTA, Marcella's teacher told Linda, "You are going to be a valuable addition to this school."

It was the first time in her life that Linda had lived in an integrated community. Linda met a neighbor, another young mother, who was black. Ethel had three children and no water. Her landlady sent her cheery postcards from Florida, where she wintered. The landlady didn't hesitate to go to Florida after hearing the news that the well for her rental house wasn't working. Ethel told Linda, "I carry water from my neighbor when she'll let me and take my laundry to Mom's house.

She was trying to make do with the three young children. Linda started carrying Ethel's laundry home to her house to do for her.

Freddy asked her, "How did the back of the car get wet?"

Linda crossed her fingers and said, "Um, I'm not sure." She was afraid to tell him. She was a little ashamed of herself; she knew that she was too helpful.

One night Ethel had a prayer meeting at her house and Linda went. The preacher spoke and the assembled, sitting in all of the dining room chairs, would say, "I believe." They said it over and over. Linda did too.

When Ethel and her husband finally found a different house to rent, Linda helped her move and clean the new house. At one point in the clean-up operation, Linda came halfway down the stairs, looked at Ethel and said, "Lady, I want you to know, I don't do no heavy housework," and they both cracked up laughing.

◆ ◆ ◆

The children became a unit, with Marcella in the lead. Marcella would decide the day's game and assign roles, even for baby Carroll. It was good that they kept their friendship with the Lindstroms, so that sometimes Andy and Heather could go off with their peers and think for themselves.

After dinner was made and the dishes washed, when the children were ready for bed, Linda often went to evening meetings. If anyone called and asked for her, Freddy would tell them, "She is out saving the world."

Linda found that she had a way with people. She could remember names and telephone numbers so that it was easy to place calls and ask, "Irene, would you be willing to be room mother for Mrs. Marsh's fourth grade class?" or "Karen, would you bake a cake for the town Christmas party?" while she was fixing dinner or feeding the baby. She was good at figuring out who might be willing to do what, so she didn't have to waste many calls. Her telephone cord was always twisted round and round from her turns as she talked and made dinner at the same time. It made Linda feel alive to use her brain this way.

Linda also began to realize that she felt disgusted by women and their dependency on men, their lack of knowledge. Her own mother depended so much on Jean and Jim Jeff. Nancy called one night, upset and in her cups. Jim Jeff had had a lawyer draw up a contract, giving him control over her finances. She asked Freddy, "Should I sign the paper?"

Freddy answered, "Nancy, I can't say unless I have seen the contract."

So she sent the contract for Freddy to read. Linda also had an opinion. Both of their opinions were that she should not sign the contract and they told her so. Jim Jeff was furious. He felt it would be better for them all if he was managing Nancy's money.

At the town meetings there was a man who spent a lot of time looking at Linda. When he did look at her, Linda remembered she was a woman, in a pleasant way.

Her admirer had craggy looks, like a jaded writer from the 1930s. This made going to the evening meetings even more interesting and perhaps she could return home late enough to avoid sex. The man's name was Scott MacDonald.

One day in exasperation, Freddy said, "I wish I weren't married to such a dull, do-gooder housewife." The words burned into Linda's brain.

Chapter Fourteen

Linda was looking for excuses to avoid having sex. Since she had decided that she shouldn't have more babies for a while, she would have been content to give up sex altogether. She also knew that wasn't normal and she began to read every book on sex she could find. Maybe she could find out what was wrong with her, why sex had never been terribly important to her and now had become repulsive.

On a visit to her gynecologist, Linda told him, "I just don't want to have sex."

"Sometimes women have a problem with false modesty," he said.

She said, "I don't really think that's me."

He suggested, "I could write a letter to the Masters and Johnson Clinic and recommend you and Freddy for treatment."

The thought was frightening enough that when Freddy said, "We can't go; how can I go to St. Louis, so close to home, and not visit my parents?" Linda was relieved, the decision was out of her hands and she could blame him.

But she was also becoming more and more agitated. If other adults were enjoying something, she wanted to enjoy it also. One night she threw one of the sex books across the room and Freddy said, "Oh, Linda, it's not worth getting that upset!"

And she answered, "That's easy for you to say because you're getting what you want!"

And he answered her, "Who says I am?"

It didn't help their relationship when, one evening just before Freddy came home from work, there was a call from Lorraine in Missouri and Freddy's father had died suddenly. "He was cleaning up and getting ready for dinner and poker with the traveling men in the parlor this evening and visiting with me. I had just come home from school and boom, he fell flat on his face and was dead. I ran out the front door of the hotel, screaming." And she fell into crying.

Linda hung up the phone and turned to the wide-eyed children who could tell from the sound of their mother's voice that something big had happened. Linda told the children, "Your granddaddy died."

Three-year-old Andy asked, "Who killed him?"

Linda thought to herself that she probably had let him watch too much television.

Linda put on her coat and went out the front door to meet Freddy before he entered the house. She thought he might want an opportunity to compose himself before he saw the children. When he drove up, she approached the driver's side and he rolled down the window. She told him. He parked, got out, brushed past her, entered the house, patted the children on their heads and began to pack.

Freddy hurried to Missouri. He called Linda long distance, "You don't need to come out; it would be too expensive and there's nothing you can do." But Linda packed up all of the children and went anyway. She felt it was important for herself, the children, Freddy and his mother. Linda's father had been 64 years old when he died but Freddy's was only 60.

When they returned to Maryland after a week with Lorraine, Freddy was locked within himself and barely spoke to Linda." What's wrong; why won't you talk to me?" Linda hated herself for it, but she couldn't take his silence and began to make scenes. "Speak to me," she pled and then screeched.

Linda called a medical school and asked them for a reference to a psychiatrist. She alarmed herself with her own rash move—no one she knew had ever consulted a psychiatrist. "But I don't understand what is happening."

The psychiatrist told them, "Freddy's grief reaction is normal for some people and, Linda, your response to his silence is also understandable." He asked them a few other questions about their life, if they had friends. He considered their answers normal and didn't think they needed to come back. Linda was relieved to have a verbal certificate of normalcy from a professional.

For her part, Freddy's mother hated life alone. She was angry with her husband for dying and she felt unable to cope with the big, old empty hotel. She called Freddy often, crying, "You're all I have to live for."

By now the Hanrahans had saved their $1,000 dollars, bought their camping gear, booked passage on a Greek freighter and were about to leave. This was a leave-taking that Linda found hard, worse even than when she had lost Barbara. She wished that she could keep her friend in a closet and have her always where she could reach her. She knew that was an impossible fantasy. It felt as if all of her own enjoyment would go when Adriane left.

Life seemed to stretch out bleakly before her.

Chapter Fifteen

Freddy's mother went to visit her sister in Texas and, since she didn't feel up to par, she went to the doctor while she was there. The doctor discovered a lump and sent her to the hospital. She called Freddy and he went down right away. The doctor decided during an operation that the cancer was inoperable and sewed Freddy's mother back up. Freddy slept in her hospital room in a sleeping bag for two weeks. He called Linda and said, "I am coming home because I can't afford to miss any more work but mom will come and stay with us as soon as she can travel."

They had begun to see the psychiatrist again for their sexual problem a few months before. He told them, "Your problem isn't sex." This was frustrating to Linda; it certainly seemed like sex to her. If making love was revolting, what else could it be? Maybe, in another several months, he would have been able to help them to see what he thought their problem was, if it wasn't sex, but he would never get the chance.

When Freddy came home from Texas, he told Linda, "We can't go to see the psychiatrist as long as Mother is around; she mustn't know that anything is wrong."

"But, Freddy, don't you understand? If we ever needed help, we need it now."

However Linda didn't convince him and the night before his mother's arrival, without further consultation with Linda, Freddy told the doctor, "We won't be back."

Later, Linda said, "That was the exact moment in time that I gave up trying."

The town was planning a crab feast to raise money for the citizens' association and for a pre-school program, tutoring, and college grants for the black children. Scott MacDonald and Linda had been part of the planning committee. That Saturday night while Freddy and the children went to the airport to pick up his mother, Linda was dishing out potato salad and stealing peeks at Scott, who was frankly watching her from over a tub full of cold sodas and beers.

Linda had bought a new pair of jeans to wear. She had asked the saleslady, "Do you think these are too tight?"

"No," the lady answered, "but don't gain an ounce."

She didn't mind when she got home and Freddy was having a nightcap with his mother; she was able to go to bed alone with her own thoughts and fantasies. She felt like a desirable woman and that thought made her feel sexual.

The next morning, Linda went to mass; she didn't know it yet, but it would be her last time. She came home and fixed a big dinner for Freddy and his mother and the children. After dinner, she announced, "I am going to take a bike ride around town." She wheeled her bike out of the garage, across the few blocks of town, and pedaled past Scott's house, hoping he would be in the yard. He wasn't, so she doubled back to try again. When he still wasn't out on the third time around, she thought she had better go home. Linda started down the street but a voice in her head said, "If you go home, some part of you will die forever."

She turned her bike around and went down Scott's driveway and, with her heart pounding in her chest, she knocked at his door. He opened it sleepily and greeted her with open arms, as if he had been expecting her. He kissed her and told her, "This isn't bad; it will only make your marriage better."

She didn't agree with him but didn't say so; she knew what she was doing was wrong. She decided then and there that she would leave Freddy and marry Scott.

Chapter Sixteen

It never occurred to Linda to think of the possibility of an affair with Scott or anyone. While she made herself go through the motions at home, she waited for a chance to tell Freddy that there was someone else in her life. One Sunday, Freddy, annoyed at her response to something, said "You and I are skating on pretty thin ice."

And she answered, "I very well know." And then she told him, "There is someone else and I am going to marry him." She didn't say who.

Now Freddy failed her test, or maybe he already had. Freddy asked, "What will we do when our mothers come for Christmas?"

Linda answered, "I don't intend to invite my mother for Christmas."

Freddy asked, "Can we stay together long enough for my mother to spend Christmas with us since it might be her last?"

Linda agreed; it was August. She made one last appointment with the psychiatrist for herself; he advised Linda, "Don't do anything rash."

As far as Linda was concerned "not doing anything rash" was no longer an option. She had declared; it was done.

Freddy came home most nights and hung his head into his dinner plate but insisted, "We aren't going to tell the children anything yet."

Linda was trying very hard to agree to what she saw as little things, like not telling the children yet. She was getting her way with the big thing—life; so she kept it a secret and didn't insist that they tell the children. She even slept with Freddy until sometime in October; it finally occurred to her that she didn't have to if she didn't want to. He argued, "Everyone will know." But she promised to get up early in the morning and clear the bedding off the couch.

As fall wore on, Freddy came home each evening later and later and Linda was relieved to not have him around, wearing on her conscience. The Hanrahans had returned from Greece and moved to the west coast. Linda had poured her heart out to Adriane about her sexual frustrations when they returned from Greece and before they left the east coast. Adriane became concerned for Linda's mental health. They continued to write each other often. Linda anxiously awaited Adriane's letters.

Linda told Freddy, "I want to visit the Hanrahans in California, now." Freddy agreed, hoping she would change her mind about separating. Freddy and the children took her to the airport and she got on the plane carrying an amphora and wheat sieve that the Hanrahans had brought back from Greece. They hadn't had room for all of their treasures in the car when they moved across the country.

Linda had made arrangements with the Hanrahans for Scott to also visit them at the same time. She knew her family would never accept what she was doing but felt she could go on, if she had the Hanrahans' blessing. And the Hanrahans did take to Scott; he was as unhampered by anyone's rules but his own, as they were.

When she returned, Freddy had a lawyer draw up a contract that was decidedly in his favor. He would let Linda live in the house until she remarried and then it was all his; he would take the investments. He would pay $250 a month in child support and an additional $125 alimony for eighteen months. He gave Linda the children, which were after all what she wanted, and one car. Linda showed the agreement to Scott and he said, "I think you can get by on it, but just barely."

Linda felt pretty guilty and decided the contract was the price she would have to pay for being untrue to her marriage; she also believed that someday a judge, granting a divorce, would say, "This agreement isn't fair," and even things up. So she signed.

And, besides, there was Daddy's money which was now Mama's money and someday it would be hers and Jean's money and then everything would end up okay.

At Thanksgiving, when Freddy took the children to visit his mother's sister, Linda visited her mother. Linda told her mother, "I've met another man. "

Nancy told her daughter, "You must have inherited a bad seed from your father. He always had other women."

Maybe, thought Linda to herself, that was why her mother had cried out "Oh, Jerry" in the middle of the night more than once, over the years.

Jean said, "All of that's nonsense," but Jean needed to believe that such things didn't happen. Linda now knew that they could.

Christmas came and Linda couldn't think of any way to explain to Marie what had happened in her life so she just signed her Christmas card "love, Linda." Freddy found an apartment. The end of the Beatles and 1970 came on December 31st.

They sat down to tell the children during the first week of January. Linda told them, "Your father and I are separating." When Marcella burst into tears on hearing this, Linda said to her, "You all can spend the night with your father some-times in his new apartment."

Freddy said, "I will thank you to let me do my own inviting." In spite of the tears, on the day their father moved, Marcella was excited because she was going to finally get her own bed-room, her parents' old room. She was ten years old. There was hardly a decent pause between her father moving out his belongings and Marcella bringing her own into the bedroom.

Linda let Freddy take some of the furniture from her family and made him some of his favorite casserole.

Chapter Seventeen

Linda went back to college with two thousand dollars her father had invested in common stock in her name when she was a child. She decided to get a teaching degree since that was what she was closest to earning, with the credits she had. There was the problem of child care. When their school let out, because of the lack of money, Linda felt she had no choice but to leave Marcella alone with Andy, eight, and Heather, six, during the mornings she was in class. "Now here's the neighbor's phone number," she told Marcella every morning as she was leaving. "Don't leave the yard or turn on the stove."

She could only afford day care for Carroll, who came home singing "We shall overcome" and some nursery songs.

Marcella and Heather continued to ask their mother, "Why don't you love daddy anymore?"

One night Heather sat and stared at Scott and said "I like you; I hate you; I like you, I hate you…"

Carroll, now four years old, had never seemed to form a close relationship with her father. As if she was reflecting her mother's growing indifference, she would walk off and ignore him when he called to her but, oddly enough, she would go up to all kinds of men who were strangers and grab them around the leg. She said nothing now that he was gone.

Andy would come up to his mother for reassuring hugs but refused to let her kiss him good-night because, he said, "You kiss other people."

She asked him, "How long would it take me to purify, if I

gave up kissing other people?"

He said, "About a week."

Scott often came over in the evenings after the children were in bed. They talked and cooked and made love. Lovemaking became something Linda wanted to do. She would allow herself to become aroused but still had not experienced orgasm.

Scott suggested she not wear a bra. "But people will see my nipples," she protested.

"Beautiful," answered Scott.

One night she felt sad when she thought Marcella spied them making love in the living room and Linda found her asleep with tears on her checks. Linda moved her own bed to a tiny room in the front of the house.

She began to try and fix things around the house. It was hard to still her mother's voice in her head that said, "You don't know anything about that!" Sometimes she had to have a good cry first and then begin the job and proceed ever so slowly. One day her mother called while she was using Scott's electric chain saw to cut some wood for the fireplace. Nancy was horrified, "I want you to get a man to do that for you. Doesn't one of your friends have a husband that would come do that?"

"Mom, how long do you think they would be friends if I borrowed their husbands?" That summer of '71 Scott and Linda took all their children, hers and his, to Maine. With seven children in tow, they looked almost like a normal family. Linda had never been to Maine. Scott arranged with his ex-wife's family to use their cabin on a lake.

There were squabbles among the children. Scott's three children ended up with separate beds of their own while three of Linda's four had to share a bed and Andy had to sleep in a sleeping bag on the floor. Linda felt that wasn't fair but she let it pass. They were able to swim and boat on a clear lake and pick blueberries. Andy paired up with Scott's son, Forrest, who was a little older. Scott also had a son the same age as Carroll who had never known his parents as anything but divorced.

That fall Linda took an art class offered by another divorced mother, who was an artist in the same small community. Linda proved to herself that she could draw, quickly sketching Scott one evening while they talked. She felt good enough about the drawing to frame and give it to him. She needed to prove to herself that she was creative. Her head was still filled with her mother's telling her over the years, "My mother could really paint; Marcella is just like her," or "My sister could really play the piano, never had a lesson; she played at the silent movies, you know."

When Linda said, "I can play the piano, Mom."

Her mother answered, "Well, that's just because your father and I bought you those expensive lessons."

Linda learned that Scott's early life had been rough. "My parents separated while I was still a baby. My mother and I moved from our expensive apartment near Central Park into her family home." The story sounded like it had been borrowed from Moss Hart's "You Can't Take it with You," with lots of eccentric aunties and uncles living together.

"My mother was usually drunk and my aunties and uncles barely noticed me. I got on my tricycle and rode off in search of my old German nanny and her husband in New Jersey. The police picked me up and helped me to complete my journey since no one reported me missing."

"When I was eight my father returned, after I hadn't seen him for six years, to pick me up and bring me to live with him and his new wife, because she hadn't been able to get pregnant. A doctor had recommended bringing another child into the house. It worked. She was able to get pregnant and had a boy and girl and then I became the family valet."

After age eight, Scott never saw his mother again. As a youngster Scott would go into empty churches and sit and ask God, "What is wrong with me?" His father lost all of his money when Scott was a teenager and never seemed to recover; he was not able to support his family. Scott vowed, "That will never happen to me." He put himself through college. When Linda met him, he was an economist who had worked for a Congressional committee but had lost his job.

"This was after I circulated a paper by a journalist which implicated Uncle Sam was still ripping off Indian water rights. I was blackballed on the hill and looking for work, not just any work. I wanted something in my field." Meanwhile, he borrowed money to live. At the point he met Linda, he owed about $25,000. In spite of all this, Scott seemed to love life.

Linda's mother came to meet Scott that same summer. "Why did you let Freddy take those good chairs?" she asked Linda. Nonetheless, she and Freddy enjoyed talking to each other on the telephone like old friends. Linda felt there was no way she could please her mother.

After the visit, Nancy went home to Kansas City to have a kidney removed, a price for all of the whiskey she had drunk. Jean and Jim Jeff had persuaded her to move from the big house into a luxury apartment but they couldn't get her to go out and have fun. She showed no interest in other men, "Why would I want another man?" she asked, "I have plenty of money."

Jean and Jim Jeff came to meet Scott the summer of '72. They were then going to go on south to visit Jim Jeff's family. By then Linda had a lawyer and Jim Jeff went with her to visit the lawyer, of whom he approved.

"She's a clean desk lawyer; that means she stays up with her work." He also tried to talk to Linda about sexuality, "Unless your sister is in the mood, I might as well forget it."

Linda had become increasingly upset again because she was aroused but never experienced orgasm. She was touched that her brother-in-law was trying to help her.

When Jean and Jim Jeff pulled out of Linda's driveway on their way south, Linda saw her situation with their eyes— too little money, a relationship with a man who was terribly in debt, four children with real needs and she became frightened.

Chapter Eighteen

Linda had returned to thinking about the Masters and Johnson Clinic in St. Louis that her doctor had suggested a couple of years before. She had been so sure that changing male partners would give her orgasms, but it didn't. She was sure that it would take nothing short of the Masters and Johnson Clinic. She learned that they wouldn't take her unless she was divorced. She chose her "clean desk" lawyer with an eye to getting divorced as soon as possible and forfeited trying to even up the division of property.

But where to come up with $2,500 for the clinic? Scott would go with her but he had no money. She asked her mother, "Mama, can I have $2,500 to go to the Masters and Johnson clinic?"

"What's Masters and Johnson Clinic?" asked Nancy.

It was difficult to explain to her mother why she needed the money. The only time she ever remembered her mother saying the word "sex" was when she said, after her father died, "I loved your father, none of that silly sex stuff, but I loved your father."

Nancy discussed Linda's request with Jean and Jim Jeff and they called and told Linda, "That clinic is a racket."

But, then, Nancy told Linda that she could have the money.

Then Scott started doing strange things. When Linda called him to tell him her mother would give her the money, he said, "It's over..." just like that, no explanation. And he hung up.

She wasn't going to let him get rid of her, Linda thought to herself. She went to his house; he wasn't home. She went in anyway and saw an untouched jug of Gallo burgundy wine sitting on the kitchen counter. She decided to drink the whole thing. About a third of the way into the bottle, she began to throw up in the shower stall off the kitchen and then passed out.

Apparently this worked to persuade Scott that she loved him because, after he found her passed out in his shower stall, he took care of her and didn't say anything else about breaking up, for a few weeks.

Then she walked in his back door one day. He sat with an array of empty beer bottles before him, glaring at her and not answering her questions.

Linda went home and called the Hanrahans in California for an interpretation of what was happening, "Why does Scott keep breaking up with me?"

Adriane asked her, "What do you expect when you keep acting the way you do?"

Linda realized with a shock that Scott had told them about her irrational behavior but not his and, worse, they believed him. This wasn't fair; they were her friends. She had introduced him to them. She needed them on her side. She was furious with him. Crazily, she dropped the phone and left it off the hook, her children watching television, and ran across the few blocks of snow in her bare feet.

"I won't let him get rid of me; he can't just drop me," she muttered to herself; she felt like a child who had been deserted in the median of a freeway. She went in Scott's back door. He was sleeping. Linda picked up a butcher knife from the counter. She ran up the stairs to where he was sleeping. She wanted to scare him, but not really hurt either one of them.

"Hey, what the hell are you doing?" Scott said as he woke, grabbed her arm and took the knife. Linda was relieved, but in the struggle, she was able to kick out the window with her bare foot and it felt good.

Afterwards, Adriane said "Don't you ever leave me hanging on the phone like that! You know, there are some things you can do to a friendship that you can never undo. You should check yourself into a hospital."

Linda's anxiety began to manifest itself in a strange fantasy, over and over. Driving along in her old car, she would see a small animal dart out in front of her wheels and it would be too late for her to stop. She would hit and crush the animal. Although it wasn't really happening, Linda was filled with anxiety.

It was eleven p.m. and Linda felt the locomotive racing inside her, carrying her along with the power to smash her into a stone wall. She wanted to talk to someone, but she felt as if there was no one. "I can't call any friends, it's so late; I can't call Mama or Jean, they'd never understand," she told herself as she tried to figure out what to do.

When she did call, her mother asked her, "What do you expect, after what you did? You left your marriage, got mixed up with that man; he's no good."

More than once, she thought about killing herself. It seemed that there were only negatives in life; but then she would put it off for a day. She would ask herself "How can I kill myself and leave my children to face life alone with the message that life isn't worth it?"

And then, on the other hand, she would ask herself, "How could I take their lives, so they wouldn't have to face life without me?" The questions kept her busy enough that she didn't do anything.

One night she dreamt she was wandering through an empty house but it was filled with a rumor. The rumor was that Freddy was dead and she had killed him. She was filled with sorrow.

In the daytime, Linda struggled to care for the children.

Andy and Heather were still friends with the Lindstrom children. Linda had introduced Scott to Eric Lindstrom, who had also split up with his wife. At first Scott and Eric seemed to enjoy each other. She asked Eric, "Do you ever think about killing yourself?"

Although Jeannie had asked him for the divorce and he had even had to live in his van for a while, he answered "No, I've never thought about killing myself."

When Eric was coming over to return her children, Linda called Scott, "Come on over; Eric is coming."

But Scott didn't show up. When she asked why, Scott answered, "Eric doesn't notice anyone else when you are around."

Linda had never realized that Eric noticed her that way, but now it dawned on her that she, too, had always been attracted to Eric.

◆ ◆ ◆

Linda finished her degree by student teaching but turned down the offer to teach at that school. "It's too far to commute every day." She was oblivious to the hundreds of applicants for every teaching job in 1972. So she had to make do with teaching poorly paid nursery school. Some weeks she had to stretch $17 to feed five people. Linda remembered Adriane's comment about "Being poor is a challenge but sometimes you get tired of the challenge."

The children began to think of themselves as poor although Linda never thought of herself that way, only short of money right now.

The divorce came through. No judge said the agreement with Freddy was unfair. Linda knew she was guilty and should suffer, but neither she nor Freddy had stopped to think their children weren't.

Chapter Nineteen

With the divorce final, money to pay the clinic and four families lined up, each to take a child for two weeks, Linda set out to drive to St. Louis to the Masters and Johnson Clinic and meet Scott who was coming in from the west where he had some work with an Indian tribe. At last, she was going to the place where everything would be made right. She didn't mind that she had to stop every two hundred miles and add oil and water to the old station wagon.

Before she left, her mother had said, "Take some man who knows something about cars, not Scott, and go get a good used car to make the trip. I'll give you the money."

But Linda changed the carburetor with a neighbor's help and drove the old car, feeling like she had already taken enough of her mother's money and wanting so desperately to prove that she could do something by herself.

The therapists assigned to them were Dr. Masters and Mrs. Biggs. Different couples had different therapists and they were just lucky to get Dr. Masters. He had eyes that looked like they could pierce steel and he was a no-nonsense man. They went through thorough physicals, and then were assigned by Dr. Masters and Mrs. Biggs to go back to the hotel and practice certain sensual exercises, no intercourse, just assigned exercises.

But they fought. Scott walked out and disappeared for several hours. Linda was furious, crying and cursing, fighting the fear that their trip to Mecca might not work.

Every day they watched the Watergate hearings on television; Scott had an intense interest in them. He said, "I hate that son-of-bitch." He told Linda a story about what Nixon had done to Helen Gahagan Douglas.

They toured St. Louis, went up in the arch, ate at some good restaurants. Linda picked out small gifts for the children. She called them and felt bad at hearing Caroll's little lonesome voice, "Mama, when are you coming home?"

She bought Raggedy Ann and Andy dolls for her.

When they returned to the clinic daily with excuses why their assignments were not done, Dr. Masters commented that he and Mrs. Biggs were dealing with "not one, but two adolescents." That certainly fit right in with Linda's belief that she could do nothing right. Dr. Masters tried to help her feel better about herself by pointing out, "Just look in any mirror." But that didn't make her feel better; what she looked like was nothing to her credit, just an accident of her birth.

Two weeks passed with no visible progress. At the last session, Dr. Masters looked surprised when Linda said, "Thank you, Dr. Masters, for studying the field of sexuality." She remembered all those years before when she had first heard of his research and how strange it had seemed. Maybe if he hadn't started it she would never have known what her problem was, but she was sure that she would have known that she had a problem.

He stated, "The treatment failure is mine and Mrs. Biggs." But Linda knew that this was for them just one of many cases, some of them successes. She was left with herself, the only one she had. She felt as if she had hit bottom and might stay there. She knew she never would have believed that the St. Louis clinic wouldn't fix her if she hadn't come and found out on her own.

Scott flew back to Arizona. Linda drove home from St. Louis in 19 hours without stopping, except to eat and, a couple of times, to sleep an hour at a rest stop.

When she walked in, the house was full of fleas; the children's beloved dog had run away from the couple that was caring for him. Heather had moved herself from the friends who were caring for her to her best friend's house; she thought her mother was in Louisiana and had set out on her bike. Carroll had a miserable two weeks terrorized by a big dog and Andy had not eaten much more than potato soup because his best friend's dad had lost his job. Linda, thoroughly chastened, decided to devote the rest of her life to her children.

One night soon after, while Linda was sleeping lightly she heard footsteps come down the hall and go out the front door. She heard her child's voice call "Mom!" and ran back to Marcella's room to find her shaking. Marcella had awakened and felt a presence beside her bed. She reached out, thinking it was the dog, which had been found, "I touched somebody; it was a man."

Linda called the police. They were still there at 2 a.m. when Scott called from Arizona. One of the police answered, thinking his call to the station was being returned. When Scott heard a man's voice, he hung up.

Linda called in a panic, "Scott, the police... "

Bang, he hung up again.

He had made it very clear to her that the one thing he wouldn't take was being cuckolded. Shortly after that night Eric Lindstrom called and asked Linda, "Will you go out to dinner with me?"

Scott still wasn't speaking to her. She told Eric she would go. They had a lovely time and ended up making love.

Then terror set in. She was afraid of Scott and afraid of losing him. She even called the therapists in St. Louis, who had told Scott and Linda that they would answer questions for a while; they said something about taking responsibility for herself.

It seemed there was nothing that anyone else could do for the mess she was making of her life.

PART THREE

Chapter Twenty

When Scott returned to town and decided to speak to her again, he asked her if she would marry him. She said yes, thinking to herself that marrying Scott would make everything that had gone before all right.

Linda quit thinking about killing herself. In later years, she thought Scott's proposal might have been just enough of a reach in her direction to make all the difference.

Meanwhile, two friends recommended her for a job at the recreated eighteenth century Quail Creek Historical Farm. It paid better than the nursery school where she had been working and she walked in and got the job. Whatever was going on in her personal life, she realized that she was still an intelligent, attractive woman who could make a good impression.

Marcella was scheduled for the last of her burn repair operations at Johns Hopkins Hospital. Somehow, over the years, they had worked in six operations. Freddy and Linda managed, in this one area at least, to behave as responsible parents. His insurance covered most of the expenses and one of them was always with her in the hospital when she was smaller, never leaving her alone. Marcella said, "If I ever get out of the hospital, I'm never coming back. I'd never be a doctor or a nurse!"

One morning before Linda started the job at the historical park, when the younger three children were leaving for school, Linda and Scott told them, "We are going to get married today before Mom takes Marcella to Baltimore to the hospital for her operation. When you get out of school, you need to go to Scott's. Heather, you get Carroll and walk her home." Linda felt some embarrassment before her children, not to mention the world. They were fully aware that the relationship with Scott was off and on, again and again.

Scott and Linda went to the courthouse to get married; Marcella sat on a bench and tried to be somewhere else.

After the courthouse marriage, Scott went back to his house and Linda drove Marcella to the hospital and stayed with her until nightfall, making it home after the others had returned from school to Scott's house. Feeling guilty that she hadn't been there to greet them, Linda asked, "How was school? I'll make us some dinner."

"Mommy, why do you have to go to the hospital with Marcella? She's a big girl," said Carroll. Heather had gone up the street to visit with her best friend, Peggy Sue.

The house was about the same size as their old one except that Andy would have to make do with a room that was really a dining room; Heather and Carroll would share a bedroom; and Marcella would have her own. Tuesday, Linda went back for the operation and sat in the waiting room, stitching on the historical costume for her new job, while waiting for the surgeon to come out with his report that everything had gone very well.

Wednesday, she brought Marcella's best friend with her to visit her at the hospital. The old station wagon stalled. She and Marcella's twelve-year-old friend pushed it through downtown Baltimore to get it started. At home later in the evening, Linda rushed around trying to paint and fix up Marcella's room for her homecoming.

It made Linda sad that fall, when Scott had a blow-up with his older son, who had become a friend of Andy's. She knew that having a step-brother close to his age would help answer Andy's desire to have a brother. Scott said, "I won't allow Forrest to come back until he apologizes." No doubt, thought Linda, Scott saw himself in his son and wasn't going to let him make the same mistakes. Forrest never apologized and Andy lost the opportunity for a brother. And, because of his mother's marriage to Scott, Andy wasn't likely to see Eric Lindstrom's son again either.

Some days were fine. But other days made Linda freeze with fear when she came home from work and found that, although things were fine when she left in the morning, by late afternoon Scott was angry with her. He would sit glaring, beside him were several empty beer bottles on the table. When she asked, frightened, "What's wrong?" He would brush past her to go sleep it off, without answering. Or worse, he accused her of finding another man. No matter what she did, Scott found a way to be angry. She had worked at the historical farm for several weeks when she decided that her second marriage had been a bad mistake. She asked her new boss, Elizabeth, for the weekend off so she could go home and leave her husband. She called Freddy to ask if she could go back to the old house, but when she opened her mouth to talk, she couldn't speak. She had no intention of crying, but she did. The last thing she wanted was Freddy's sympathy.

Freddy said "Of course, stay as long as you need."

When she told Scott what she intended to do, he seemed to not care but as she was gathering up the children and some belongings, he said "Leave, now!"

Linda said, "No, not until I get our clean clothes out of the drier."

Scott said, "NOW" and followed her to the basement. Linda began to pull clothes from the drier. Scott took hold of her long hair and started to pull. Linda planted her feet, determined to hold her ground.

Just then, the children came to the basement door. Marcella, who never learned to call Scott by his given name said "Mr. MacDonald, let go of my mother." Scott came to his senses, turned and left them. Linda packed the children into the old station wagon and pulled out of the driveway with several mattresses, some clothes, the dog and $17. Over the weekend, Linda borrowed $300 from friends to put a down payment on a rental house and called various clinics that worked with alcoholics to see what she should do. All advised her, "Don't return until your husband promises to get help."

When she talked with him, he said, "You come back and then I'll get help."

Linda stared into the fire she had built in the fireplace. They were sleeping in the living room at the old house. She looked at her children's sweet heads as they lay sleeping on mattresses on the floor. "Dear God, what should I do?" was her prayer of desperation. In the morning, she decided to stick with the marriage, make it work. On Sunday, she went back to Scott's house and returned the $300 to her friends.

Scott agreed to see a therapist who stated firmly, "I can't work with you unless you totally give up all alcohol." It helped to get Scott's cooperation that the therapist was a Native American. He bought a case of soda and kept one in his hand at all times. Life began to settle down.

◆ ◆ ◆

Working in the eighteenth century setting gave Linda an opportunity to use some of her hidden talents, sewing and decorating the period clothing, cooking over the fireplace. Her only problem was looking too healthy. All those spoonfuls of cod liver oil that her mother had put into Linda's mouth when she was a child left her with a body and face that radiated health, hardly appropriate for the hardships of eighteenth century life. Linda read firsthand accounts of the life so that when people asked her questions she could do a little gentle history teaching. One of the questions one day was, "What did mothers, who were always so busy, do with their toddlers?"

Linda thought about it, "Maybe sometimes the mothers would have to tie their child into a chair, since there was certainly no baby furniture in the average eighteenth century house."

Her farm spouse, a lazy but affable fellow, would listen to Linda and copy her answers. When she heard him tell a visitor, "The eighteenth century family tied their children in chairs," she grabbed the hoe and stormed out of the cabin. Out to the fields she marched, with the heavy iron hoe, before she could bring it down on his head. She was hitting angrily at the ground when she noticed a tall middle-aged man motioning to her from the rail fence.

"What do you suppose this farmer's political sentiments would have been at this point in time, right before the American Revolution?" he asked her.

Linda answered, "I don't know, but why don't you go into the cabin and ask that fellow; he'll tell you even if he doesn't know."

Later Linda learned that the man was in charge of all their region for the park service. Laughingly, she asked, "Hey, Joe, do you know what I did to you?"

One day she found herself knowing how to clean a chicken, the memory drawn from her childhood: into the boiling water, rub off the feathers, cut off the head, reach into the cavity, cut open the gizzard and rinse it out. She must have been no more than three or four years old when she watched her mother and aunt doing this.

Linda found that she was good at telling people about life from so long ago and she was willing to work to redeem herself. She found herself thinking how hard life must have been as she raised the iron hoe over her head and brought it down between the rows in the kitchen garden. Sometimes she just lay down on the soft, loose, black earth in the sunshine and closed her eyes.

There were late afternoons when she and Elizabeth would

sit under the trees and sip lemonade from ceramic mugs and swap family stories, some going back to the "recent unfortunate trouble between the states" as their families had referred to the Civil War. It was not so recent as to not be funny now.

She didn't change from her costume at the end of the day because it would have meant just that much more laundry for her to do. She lay, almost asleep, in her petticoat, bodice and shift in front of the fire at home as the children asked her questions about their homework. "Mom, what's five times seven?"

Linda worked every weekend. The children spent weekend after weekend without their mother unless they wanted to visit the site, don costumes and spend the day in prerevolutionary America. Sometimes they did. One day Heather helped her mother and Elizabeth pick tiny little ripe wild strawberries. They washed them and set them on the table in the cabin. They tasted so good and sweet that Linda kept coming back for a few more until they were all gone. Heather returned to get a few and when she saw they were all gone, said, understandingly, "I guess Mommy's been here." Elizabeth, watching from the window, chuckled to herself.

Elizabeth was accepting of Linda; she knew Linda didn't mind using the woods for a lavatory but that she loved to keep a twentieth century cola in the trees or behind the door of the cabin.

Linda asked Scott "Would you help the children with their homework?" since she had to be gone all weekend. Sometimes he said he would but never got around to it. Only Heather was doing very well in school.

Scott did do the cooking occasionally. The children didn't spend much time with Freddy. He would ask them to a concert or museum but their childish tastes didn't run along those lines and Freddy didn't care to change his.

When she wasn't in the eighteenth century, Linda was working on Scott's house. A charming stucco from the 20s, set on a large wooded lot, Scott had not had money to keep it up and he didn't do the things that he could have done on his own, such as painting. Linda set out to scrub all of the interior walls that had darkened over the years with smoke from the fireplace and Scott's cigarettes. She knew that her mother was coming for Christmas and, while she would never be able to improve the house to her mother's standards, she might be able to get it up to her own. Then she would be able to ignore it when her mother said what Linda knew she would say.

Linda hadn't written Marie in years; they had only exchanged cards. Linda was ashamed of her life but this year she wrote a little note on her Christmas card to Marie

Christmas 1974

Dear Marie,
  My Mom's coming to visit this year with Kathy, Jean's daughter, for Christmas. I'm working in the 18th century. What's up with you and yours?

Love,
Linda

Kathy was the redhead that had been substituted when heaven was out of boys. Linda was very glad to see them as they came down the ramp from the plane. She drove Nancy and Kathy and the children around the big national Christmas tree that night to see the bright lights and decorations. The next day Kathy came with Linda to the farm to feed the animals. No one else was working. Laughing, they tossed hay to the cattle and Linda climbed in the pen with the little pig who seemed to be squealing from lonesomeness. On Christmas Eve, they sat around the Christmas tree, Nancy with a drink in her hand, listening to the grandchildren talking excitedly. Nancy tried to give a five dollar bill to Scott's younger son, "Here, Sweetie, I want you to have this; you're such a nice boy."

Scott frowned and called him aside. He made the boy refuse the money. "You tell Mrs. Jones that's very nice but you cannot keep it."

This made Nancy, who had been drinking all evening, very angry. Linda felt caught between the two. At almost midnight, her mother went into the kitchen to clean the turkey while Linda was putting the children to bed. After the last cheek was kissed, Linda came into the kitchen and saw her, she said, "It's okay, Mama, I'll do that tomorrow."

Nancy could still stand up only by leaning her arms on the edge of the kitchen sink, but she said stubbornly "I'm gonna do it now!"

Linda looked over at the stove. "Mom, you have the giblets boiling in their plastic bag, and you've got too much margarine in a pan set on a burner turned too high." Linda thought about the fire that could start with all of that fat and she exploded. "Mama, go to bed! I'll do this tomorrow." Linda took hold of her mother and tried to lead her to the bedroom, but Nancy wouldn't budge. Linda heard herself screaming "You're going to bed!" as she tried to push her mother into the bedroom. Then, when Nancy was still immobile, Linda raised her hand and hit her mother. Kathy and Scott stood outside of the room, waiting and listening. The children were in bed but they heard too. Linda turned and fled to her bed where she collapsed in tears.

After her grandmother was asleep, Kathy hid the whiskey bottle in the downstairs shower. The next day, Christmas, Nancy seemed considerably chastened. She and Linda didn't talk about what had happened just as no one had ever discussed the Christmases in Kansas City when Nancy would work for days in the kitchen, preparing for the twenty-fifth, letting no one help her. Then, just as the family sat down to eat, she had to go to bed, exhausted and drunk.

She would revive in time to clean the kitchen; of course, no one else could do it the way she wanted.

Nancy and Kathy flew back to Kansas City the day after Christmas and Nancy never came to visit Linda again.

Chapter Twenty One

The second year that they were married, Scott began to drink again. A beer now and then evolved into a six pack from time to time and then, finally, he drank again all of the time, every day, except when he was asleep.

Briefly, Linda actually felt ashamed when he accused her, "You're so goal-oriented." One of her goal's was trying to keep him from getting deeper into debt. When Scott couldn't pay the mortgage, she did. She was trying not to lose this house. She had already lost one house, giving it to Freddy to make up for her sins.

Nancy Jones said repeatedly to Linda, "You were so stupid to give that house to Freddy," but she also made it clear to Linda that she thought Linda was guilty. No matter how hard she tried, there was no way for Linda to do the right thing in her mother's or Scott's eyes. Linda's frustration fed her anger.

One time Linda was so angry with Scott that she said, "I want to kill you," and she meant it. He believed her and left for a whole weekend without saying where he was going. She sat under a tree and asked herself later, "Why did I want to kill him?" She realized it was because she felt nothing else that she could do or say would have any effect on him. She felt powerless.

Scott's house wasn't really hers to hold onto; it actually belonged to Scott and his first wife.

When Linda talked to Scott about putting the house into both of their names, he evaded her or said, "I can't do it because of all the money I owe," or "I'm not going to disinherit my children."

Around the corner, there was a small frame house for sale. It had been on the market quite a while, so long that the owner left the empty house unlocked so that prospective buyers could let themselves in to see it. One night, as Marcella was coming back from a babysitting job, Linda met her in the street and said, "Come on in, I'll show you a house that I might buy."

The house was essentially four rooms and it was inexpensive."Ma, there's no way we would fit in this house."

So Linda answered Marcella, "Just you watch."

Linda fantasized moving into the house and staying friends with Scott. The two of them would help each other out, but she would be putting her money into a home of her own. She still didn't have any money, so she asked her mother yet again. "Mom, I am thinking about moving out of here and I need some money to put a down payment on a house. Can you give me about ten thousand?"

Nancy Jones said, "I'll have to think about it." Probably important in her final decision to do it was the fact that Nancy couldn't stand Scott.

When Linda called the real estate agent, he must have heard the uncertainty in her voice and he urged her to be sure.

She told Scott, "I asked Mama for money to buy the little frame house around the corner. We can still be friends and help each other out from different houses."

It all took three months to complete. During those months, Linda often burst into tears. Little Carroll sat on her mother's lap and cried too. But Scott didn't cry or talk about it. He drank and slept and stayed away from home more and more.

She and the children had good neighbors here. Across the street, two artists bought a little ramshackle house that had been condemned by the county and lived there surreptitiously while they repaired it. They reminded Linda a little of the Hanrahans and she became good friends with

Cynthia, the common-law wife.

At last the weekend arrived. Cynthia said, "I can't help on Saturday or Sunday, but I want come over and help you get started on Friday night."

"No, that's all right, Cynthia. We'll manage. Please don't feel like you have to help."

But Cynthia said, "I'll be there."

She was there late Friday afternoon when Scott came in the back door and began furiously to tell Linda, "I'm not going to let the neighbor children in this yard and you had better let them know." He worked to a higher and higher pitch and Linda was pretty sure that he would have hit her if Cynthia hadn't walked into the kitchen from the living room. Scott turned on his heel and left, staying away that night and the next.

Linda and the children hurried to fill the car so that she could drive around the corner to the new house with the load. The children walked, carrying and pulling still other belongings. Andy was a big help but the two older girls had just been ill and couldn't help much. Back and forth, countless times, until Sunday noon when they were down to the last few loads. Linda spied Scott walking back through his yard with angry eyes. Into the house he went, and slammed the door, and Linda drove away, saying a silent goodbye to the remainder of her possessions.

When she and Freddy separated, people had asked, "Why did you leave him?"

But when she left Scott, people asked, "Why did you marry him?

Chapter Twenty Two

L inda made up her mind that she would never move again, now that she had her own house. The first bills paid every month were for the first and second mortgage. Whatever was left over from her paycheck, and it wasn't much, would cover food, utilities, and, if they ever got that far down on the list, clothes. Linda's friends were tired of hearing, "I bought these pants at the Methodist church rummage sale."

Marcella worked long hours after school in the day care center to afford two pair of designer jeans, which dried in the oven while breakfast was being eaten. They didn't have a drier; the wiring in the house was too old. Besides Linda noticed how much lower the electric bill was without one.

There were only two bedrooms in their new house. Linda said to Marcella, "You can have the biggest bedroom; who do you want for a roommate, Heather, Carroll or me?"

Marcella said, "Heather." It was a good choice; it had always seemed to Linda that Marcella and Heather were a pair, and Andy and Carroll were a pair.

Linda joked, "Maybe one set is from the right ovary and the other from the left."

Linda moved into the smaller bedroom with Carroll and made a small place for Andy's bed off the kitchen. Unfortunately, most of Andy's toys and other belongings had to go to the basement but, nonetheless, on their first night in the new house, Andy said to his mom as she was tucking him in, "I guess this house isn't so bad after all." The children were all glad to have Scott out of their lives.

Now that she was a homeowner, Linda would walk through the aisles of hardware stores with a brand new interest. "There's a tool to do that job...," she thought to herself. It wasn't some kind of a mystery that was beyond all females. She could fix things. She had come a long way since Scott taught her the difference between a screw and a bolt.

One day, rather than buying a closet pole she cut down a broom handle to put up as a bar in Marcella and Heather's closet. After the girls had loaded on all of their clothes, the broom handle broke.

"Goddamn, Freddy!" Linda exploded. Marcella and Heather watched their mother silently. Linda sat back on the bed and realized she was angry at Freddy because she was always short of money. She had given Freddy the house and money so she wouldn't have to feel guilty but it hadn't worked, she still felt guilty and, on top of that, angry. Now she had put up the broom handle to save money and it was not thick enough.

"Okay, girls, I'll get a closet rod."

Linda realized that she needed a job with more income. Cynthia had told her about a job opening closer to home. The park service was looking for someone to operate an art gallery in a closed amusement park that had become an arts center. It would mean working on weekends still but, in a way, that was good. It kept her from spending too much time with herself; the thought of just being alone scared her. The drawback was more time when the children wouldn't have any adult at home. Linda went in to try for the job. She knew the arts center manager, having met him at Quail Creek several times and he hired her on the spot.

Linda saw River Cliffs Park as Brigadoon, a place from another time, set down in the midst of everyday life. The park had been built in 1891 as a Chautauqua; later it became an amusement park. In the middle of the park, there was a carousel and around the carousel revolved a century's assortment of buildings.

There was still an immense ballroom from the roaring twenties. Inside you could smell the memory of couples dancing to the Charleston, the Lindy, the jitterbug, while Benny Goodman played "Sing, Sing, Sing" in the background. Linda knew that if someone led her around the park blindfolded, she would recognize this building by its smell.

During the 1950s, many of the folks who bought cars after World War II wanted to drive their cars out of town to the new theme parks springing up in the countryside. In the 1960s, River Cliffs was going downhill, starting to fall apart and losing money. The owners tried to close the amusement park, knock it down, use the land more profitably. The neighbors had saved it and River Cliffs became an arts park.

Linda was determined to work hard and prove herself in her new job. She bought an old bicycle from Heather for $6 and became a familiar sight riding the mile and a half to work everyday. Twice a day, the ride was like a calming meditation.

The park manager said to her, "We've advertised that the art gallery will open in the old Chautauqua stone tower on May 19th, three weeks from now. It hasn't been used for much but storage for a decade or more. I'm not sure who's going to be getting the tower ready." The ground floor was divided into several tiny rooms filled with quantities of paraphernalia, including the six foot figure of a cowboy from the old shooting gallery, thousands of unfolded boxes from the popcorn stand, old desks, chairs, trash.

The second floor of the tower was filled with all of the metal tiles that had been removed a few years before from the roof; no one knew if they were historically important, so the tiles were saved. The tower had 144 small glass panes in its tall Victorian windows and more than half were broken. The plaster walls had holes in them. Linda saw a rat disappear into one of the holes when she opened the door.

Linda just started to shovel out the trash.

◆ ◆ ◆

She had made it through three weeks without a man in her life, after she left Scott's house. They had not stayed friends and, by then, she realized it was just as well. She could take care of herself and the children physically, but she still felt emotionally incomplete.

Linda called Eric Lindstrom with an excuse to get the boys together. The boys had never lived close enough to each other to be in control of their own relationship but needed a parent to drive them miles to the other's house, the parents who had been engaged in finding themselves. Once Andy said "Sometimes I feel like I'll never see Ricky again."

Eric and Linda came together again with a bang, born of the years of knowing and being attracted to each other. Eric told Linda, "I've loved you for fourteen years." Eric rushed her, bringing flowers and arriving early to pick her up for dates, doing the dishes if she wasn't quite ready. Spring in Washington, D.C. is a beautiful background for romance and Linda marveled how 40 felt like 16!

While Linda was working on the tower, Eric showed up some late afternoons and began to knock down the walls on the first floor with a sledgehammer. When other people saw that work was going forward, they offered to help.

Linda glazed the 70-plus broken panes in the windows; she knew how to do it because Scott had taught her to glaze after she kicked out his window. Linda painted the walls and window trim. Andy sat with Eric's son on a window sill on the second floor to pitch the metal tiles into the back of a stake body truck, Linda having made the executive decision that they weren't historically significant.

It was a frantic rush. Linda worked 20 days out of 21 to get the tower ready. She and Marcella hung the first show late the night before the gallery was to open but they made it. She continued that summer to keep the gallery open every day, day after day, a luxury that the park hadn't had before.

One of the park artists stuck her head around the door and said, "Honestly I think the gallery has become real."

Sometimes the park artists made fun of Linda's artistic ignorance behind her back, but they also taught her some of the things she needed to know. Linda wrote "sold" on the label by a painting. Natasha, the artist who had begun to drop in regularly to visit, told her about red dots.

July, 1976

Dear Marie,

It's been a long time but your mom told my mom who told me what was going on with you. I hope we can write again after so long. Please forgive me.

I have begun to study dance at age 40 and I am taking class at the writing center here in the park where I work. I am making pictures out of fabric. I love the park...

Chapter Twenty Three

In spite of the fact that Linda had called Jean before she called their mother to ask for the down payment money for this house, somehow the wires got crossed and Jean ended up angry and not speaking to Linda. Linda had a mental picture of her mother as the operator at telephone central, crossing all of the communications wires.

Something their mother said gave Jean the idea, who said to Jim Jeff, "Linda took this new job and it pays less money than her old job! She's so spoiled when it means more of Mama's money might be needed to bail her out."

However, when Jim Jeff would make a derogatory comment about Jean's sister, she would stand up for Linda and say, "Linda isn't as bad as your brother." However the sisters didn't call or write each other for more than a year. Linda missed being able to talk to Jean but she wasn't willing to be the first to break the silence.

After the first rush, there were periods when Eric didn't call. When he did, Linda asked, totally bewildered and more than a little anxious, "Why haven't you called for a week?" Then it was two weeks between calls, then more.

Eric answered "I've been busy."

Linda fantasized hurting herself to get his attention, picturing hitting her head against the stone walls of the tower. She knew that kind of thinking was sick. At home, she would hide in the basement, where she thought the children couldn't see or hear, and sob. Once she collapsed into the grass, crying, with the electric mower roaring in front of her.

Finally, there were no more calls from Eric. When she

couldn't stand it any longer, she called him early one Saturday morning. A woman answered the phone and Linda thought she had dialed the wrong number so she excused herself and tried again.

The same woman answered and Linda left a message for Eric to call her. When he did, she asked him, "There's another woman in your life, isn't there? You make me so damn mad, coming in and telling me that you love me, and just neglecting to tell me that you were already involved. I feel like coming there and throwing rocks through your windows."

He assured her, that if she did, he would call the police.

When she left Scott, Linda had told Susan, the therapist, that she could not afford to continue. Now she called Susan and asked, "Could I come back for just one visit?"

Susan said "I don't usually agree to see someone coming for just one time, but all right, we'll see what we can do."

During the visit, Susan leaned over and handed her a packet of papers, "You might want to read these lectures." After dinner, Linda sat on the porch swing and began to read them slowly, whenever she had time over weeks. She lost herself in memories from long ago that were triggered by the words she was reading. The lectures talked about how people will recreate situations that they faced as children in order to learn to deal with them as adults.

Linda called Susan and asked, "Susan, where did the lectures come from? How do I learn more?" This was her introduction to The Way; Linda joined the group which met every Monday night. It was going to cost some money.

They worked in the group by bringing up feelings and confronting them. When Linda couldn't reach her feelings, the group leader handed her a padded bat, called a bataka, and encouraged her to pound on a pillow and say the words that came up; it helped her to realize how very angry she was.

She was very proud of herself the night she picked up a bataka and fought one of the men for her turn. Linda realized that she liked some controversy, especially when she stood up for herself.

May, 1977

Dear Marie,

I needed help and I have joined a group. Since you live in California you probably have heard of this sort of thing—concept of creating your own reality and all that. It is helpful, though, to me to realize what mixtures of good and bad we all are. I don't have to feel so ashamed of myself...

Chapter Twenty Four

The children developed a routine. When they spied their mother coming home from work, they hid for the first half hour. They knew she would look at the mess and scream. So they hid instead of picking up the dishes, coats, and books.

Linda had always yelled out her frustrations at the children. Sometimes she had strayed over the line into hitting. It was always easier for her to hit Marcella and Heather, maybe because at some deep level they reminded her more of herself.

Once, when she was in the last years of being married to Freddy, her in-laws were coming for a visit. "The house has to look perfect," she told herself. As she cleaned a room, it became off limits to the children. Heather had gone back into a clean room and finger painted.

"Heather!" Linda screamed, and she spanked and spanked the child. "If you live until you're 21 and I don't strangle you!"

After she and Freddy had separated, Linda relaxed so much that she lost control over the house and its messes and was left confused, "Where to start?" she asked herself, and very often she didn't.

The other children never posed as much of a challenge as Heather. Swallowed up in the middle, she was always doing something outrageous. When she hit adolescence, Linda said to Cynthia, "God handed Heather a loaded pistol...a knockout body and face and since she hasn't had much experience with men, she doesn't know what to do with such power."

Cynthia answered, "But that won't last long."

Marcella said to her mother, "Heather's so pretty."

Linda answered, "Shall we just hate her?" But Linda worried about what might be in store for this daughter.

Marcella helped her mother get organized so that each of the children took a portion of responsibility for the housework. Marcella herself, however, was spending a certain amount of her high school years cutting classes, smoking dope, and getting sexually initiated. One morning she awoke at 5 a.m. to find Marcella not at home. It was almost too much to bear: all of the children had trouble with school; Marcella didn't talk to her; Andy didn't talk to Heather and there was still just barely enough money.

Yet it wasn't all bad in their cosy little frame house. After the kids had gone to bed, many nights Linda played the piano until she was tired herself. Carroll confessed, "I like to go to sleep listening to you play, Mom."

One night Linda looked up from playing to see Marcella holding the phone out in front of her, the cord stretched to its' limit. When Linda asked, "What are you doing?" Marcella answered, "I'm holding the phone up for Lisa my friend to hear you play the piano."

◆ ◆ ◆

"Hello," a voice answered the phone.

Linda recognized her sister's voice right away. "Hi, Jean, can I talk to you?" Linda decided that she needed to talk to her sister about life and she swallowed her pride and called.

The sisters made up. It was a comfort to be able to ask each other long distance "Why does mother say the things to us that she does?" They never came to a conclusion but it helped to not feel alone.

Jean also asked Linda, "Why do you do such bizarre things?"

Linda knew she had done some bizarre things but wasn't

sure which Jean knew about and didn't want to tell her about any she didn't already know, so she asked, "Which bizarre things?"

That Christmas, Linda bought an opal ring for her sister, made by one of the artists at the park. She bought gifts for her own children from Woolworths. Her mother sent $300 and the five of them got on a Greyhound bus and rode 30 hours to Kansas City.

As they left Washington, Heather was throwing up in a paper bag on her mother's lap. It was Linda's fortieth birthday. After Heather fell asleep, Linda and Carroll sat gazing out at the countryside at night. They made up a new rendition of "Night Before Christmas we were both on a bus..." It was the only good part of the trip for them; the other three weren't so fortunate; they didn't have any good part.

Marcella, unknown to her mother had prepared for the trip by toking up on a little marijuana. She was also throwing up in the tiny bathroom on the bus. Andy rode stoically along, letting his little sister rest her head on his lap. They were up near the front door and Linda worried about them being cold. They all arrived in Kansas City exhausted.

That night was Christmas Eve and they went with Nancy to Jean and Jim Jeff's. Jean opened the small package, "Thank you, Linda," she said as she slipped the ring onto her finger. Linda could tell that her sister really liked her gift, no small accomplishment.

When they returned to Nancy's apartment, Nancy said "I'm going to do a little cooking."

Linda groaned to herself. For a small woman, her mother could make quite a racket in the kitchen. At 3 a.m., Andy whispered, "Mom, I can't sleep."

Linda went down the hall and asked, "Mama, please go to bed now."

When her mother ignored her, Linda began to demand that Nancy go to bed.

Nancy, who was quite drunk, became angry, "Just leave my house right now."

Disgustedly, Linda answered her, "There's no way I'm going to wake these kids in the middle of the night and leave!" and she went back to bed. Nothing was said the next day and they went for turkey at Jean's.

Jean and Jim Jeff had offered, "Nancy, we'll sell you the Plymouth for a song so you can give it to Linda as her Christmas gift since her old car died." Linda and the children had been making do without a car. Nancy accepted Jean and Jim Jeff's offer.

"Thanks, Mom; we really need it," Linda meant it.

Driving the Christmas car back from Kansas City, they hit a bad snowstorm on the Pennsylvania turnpike. "I can't see anything; it looks like I'm driving off the edge of the world," Linda told the kids.

"I can do it, Ma. Let me take the wheel," Marcella told her mother. Linda hesitantly handed over the wheel and Marcella headed through the driving white. They arrived home safely.

Linda found out that the park service, while they were gone, had upgraded her job to ranger in an effort to comply with equal opportunity requirements. It had been noted that most of the ranger grade jobs were held by males, while jobs with equal responsibilities were called "park technician" and held by females. It reminded Linda of the joke about, "I couldn't use to spell it and now I are one."

◆ ◆ ◆

Marcella had begun as a teenager to talk about moving in with Freddy, who was still living nearby in their house on the river. When Marcella was younger, he had said she couldn't because he was often gone from home on business trips but now she was almost an adult. It hit Linda hard. If her daughter wanted to leave her, it meant to her that she was a failure.

Linda told Marcella, "Your father will probably make you feel bad about yourself." She really wanted to persuade Marcella not to go.

After graduation, Marcella spent the summer in California with Lisa, working at a delicatessen. She saved enough money to come back across the United States by bus with a bag of sandwiches and five dollars left over, which she spent on books. Freddy picked her up at the bus station. Linda was out in the yard when she spied Marcella walking up the street from her father's house with her little sister.

"Where are your bags?" she asked her daughter.

Marcella answered, "They're down at dad's. I'm moving in down there."

Linda felt like she had been slapped across the face. She had lost her daughter.

It was not too much later that she realized that she didn't lose anything. Her daughter began to appreciate her, became her friend.

Chapter Twenty Five

The Way took up a certain amount of Linda's life with group meetings and private sessions and, a few times a year, trips to a country place, where it was harder for her to hide from her own loneliness. Her divorce from Scott came through; this one was at her own expense.

One of her trips to The Way's country place was for a weekend devoted to working on vocations. Linda didn't think of that particular weekend as an opportunity to meet men. She knew, after she introduced herself as 40 years old with four teenagers, that no one would be interested. That night she dreamed she was wearing gloves to cover work-worn hands, like Scarlet O'Hara in *Gone With the Wind* when Scarlet was trying to present herself as desirable to Rhet Butler.

Michael approached her near the end of the weekend and admitted that he had just about convinced himself to ask her out. He was younger than Linda, had never been married and had no children; she warned him, "You'd better go home and sleep on that," and practically ran to her car.

As she drove to the city she asked herself, "Why did you do that? What are you afraid of?" and realized she was afraid of being hurt. There was an unwritten rule: younger men are not attracted to older women. Dare she challenge it? Michael already had.

After she was home, she told Marcella what had happened. "Well, you're going to go, aren't you?" Marcella asked.

Linda answered, "What would people think, a forty-year-old woman with four teenaged children, dating a twenty-eight-year old man?"

Marcella answered "Ma, that's so stupid!"

On an impulse, Linda changed her mind.She called Michael, "If you still want to go out, I would like to go."

He answered, "I feel sort of on the spot and I'll have to think about it."

Linda felt proud of herself for taking action and bet that she would never hear from him again. But two nights later, he called and asked her out.

On their first date, they went to see an obscure play at the writing center at River Cliffs Park and then back to Linda's house. The living room was furnished with a hammock, a picnic table and a piano. Linda felt she couldn't afford a couch but had bought the handmade nylon rope hammock from an artist at the park. The piano started with a $150 gift from her mother to herself and Carroll; Linda had paid the remainder slowly over a couple of years. The picnic table had been sent as a gift from her mother, the children assembled it by themselves when it arrived, since their mother wasn't home. They had no other table so they used it to dine on inside. It made a rough surface for doing homework, just one of several excuses the children had cooked up to not do their homework.

Michael was a little taken back by the furnishings. The only places to sit were the hammock and some pillows on the floor. At the end of the evening, he said, "I want to spend the night." He was annoyed when she gently shoved him out the door. "Linda, it is 1978."

Michael had grown up in the country. He was quite intelligent but his experiences had been limited. He always found himself attracted to older women. He was closer in age to Marcella than to Linda.

"When I was growing up, I hated farm work. I always

wanted to stay in the house and help my mom." His brothers had called him a sissy. "I wasn't sure that they weren't right." He had worried that he wasn't a real man.

Michael and Linda dated for a number of months before he took her to meet his family. He had already told them that she was 40 and twice divorced. It was very difficult for Linda to go.

She joked, "You are going to have to chloroform me and put me in the back of the station wagon and point to me through the window." Instead she took along some sewing that she was doing for extra cash from Quail Creek farm. She intended to keep busy, hide her face, and impress her future mother-in-law with her domesticity.

Actually, she hadn't needed to worry. Rachel and Beverly were without airs. Rachel, Michael's mother, cooked on a wood-burning stove. She agreed to Linda's offer to help then insisted that Linda sit down to eat with the rest of the family. Rachel continued to bustle about the kitchen, serving them. On the way home Linda told Michael, "I feel perfectly comfortable with your folks."

Later, at a Sunday School picnic, Beverly introduced her as his future daughter-in-law. Linda remarked to her own mother, "They seem to accept me."

Her mother answered, "Well, honey, why wouldn't they?"

Although he was usually very quiet, Michael talked enough for Linda to find out how alike they were. Each had spent a year thinking about suicide, feeling they were failures, and had sought help. Linda said, "I feel like we are in the same grade in life."

Although Michael had studied science in college, he was interested in astrology. "How will it be for two Capricorns like us to get together?" Linda asked him.

He answered, "Pretty boring." Boring seemed okay, given that each had a lot of healing to do.

Linda was conscious almost always of being older. She

worried about how she looked from a given angle, in a certain outfit. At one point, Michael seemed about to lose interest in the relationship and Linda decided on the spot to ask him to help her. It had taken her a lot of time to convince herself that she could do what she needed to do to take care of herself and her children, so it was hard to let go of the determination to do it all. Linda told herself, "Relax, you've already proven yourself." She asked Michael, "Would you like to help me fix the garage roof?"

Linda found out that Michael was a perfectionist; he was pretty horrified that she was anything but. Linda's unconscious motto was, "Get it done."

Michael's motto more matched Linda's mother's, which was "There's no point in doing something unless you do it right." For them, right meant perfectly.

The garage roof was finished—perfectly.

When they had dated almost a year, Michael asked "Do you mind if I put up shelves in front of your windows for my plants?" and that was the way that she knew he was moving into her four room house with three teens, one dog and three cats. Linda had had trouble holding the line at three, since the children always wanted to bring home more.

Linda's mother and sister had trouble accepting the fact that she was living with a man out of wedlock. In fact, when Linda and Michael traveled to Kansas City for her niece's wedding, although her mother had arranged to rent a suite for Linda and Michael, Jean insisted, "Carroll should stay with us. It's hard on mother when you live like this."

Yet the next year, when Linda was in Kansas City, Jean and Linda were visiting in the bedroom as Jean dressed. Jean had had a change of heart. Her divorced friend, Taffy, who was lonely, had gone out with a man and stayed out all night. Taffy's mother would not speak to her for months because she believed that what her daughter had done was a sin. Jean could see how lonely Taffy was and decided that, "In some cases, sex outside of marriage is okay, if both people are over 25 years old."

Jean told her little sister how, when she and Jim Jeff were with their friends, she stood up for the ERA. "I said it may be too late for us but think of younger women."

"Good for you," Linda told her sister and felt proud.

Linda noted with pleasure for her sister that after years of having a flat chest, Jean had a bosom. "Maybe this is what menopause does for you," thought Linda to herself. It was the last time the sisters were together.

In the summer of 1981, Linda woke one July morning to newspaper headlines from Kansas City. The night before free-hanging balconies in a beautiful new hotel had fallen on dancers below, crushing them as they danced to Count Basie's "Satin Doll." Linda wondered if Jean and Jim Jeff had known anyone who was there; it was the sort of music their friends would like.

Michael had begun the day preparing for the picnic he was hosting for his college alumni friends that afternoon. He was passing outside of the kitchen window with garden hose in hand and heard the phone ring. Fiona called, "Aunt Linda, Mom and Dad were at the Hyatt Regency last night."

Linda choked. She had a strange feeling that she had caused them to be there by thinking about them when she read of the disaster.

That morning the rescue workers lifted the last slab and found thirty some more bodies. Jean and Jim Jeff were among them.

Chapter Twenty Six

For the first time in her life, Linda felt sorry for her mother. Children do not die before their parents. Linda had often thought of her mother as an ostrich, hiding her head from the unpleasantness in life. "Mama, not thinking about something doesn't make it untrue," Linda would say when her mother told her that she didn't want to hear about that awful thing.

Nancy Jones had fallen asleep having convinced herself that Jean and Jim Jeff were not at the Hyatt Regency, "Thank God they weren't there," she told herself.

Fiona was not so fortunate; she knew where they were. A teenager, she had fought with her parents, even as they went out the front door. She was watching television when the program was interrupted by news of the disaster. "There has been a collapse of the sky walks at the Hyatt Regency Hotel in Crown Plaza and some of the people attending the tea dance are trapped beneath the heavy slabs of concrete. Emergency equipment and personnel are rushing to the scene..."

Several of Jean's and Jim Jeff's friends also knew where they had gone because the couple had called them, inviting them to come along to the dance. Friends soon began to arrive at the house and waited together with Fiona throughout the night. Morning came before the phone rang with news.

A close friend who was a doctor went to the temporary morgue to identify their bodies. He told them, "They had to have died instantly."

◆ ◆ ◆

Tommy, Debby, Kathy, Fiona and Linda were sitting around the living room planning the funeral. Linda thought of her sister and how she had said, "There's no point to lots of rooms, family rooms, TV rooms, formal living rooms," when they were designing the house with an architect years earlier. This big room with one wall made up of windows, still attested to Jean's good taste.

There was Jim Jeff's piano. "Remember the story when your Dad was crossing France with the invading Allied forces and he came upon an old upright in a deserted farmhouse and broke into a boogie-woogie while heavy shooting was going on outside?" Linda asked the others.

"They were going to join his old Army buddies next summer for a reunion in Europe," Debbie answered.

Tommy had become a musician himself. "I was playing yesterday and I looked up and saw Dad watching through the window. How about 'When the Saints Go Marching In' for the funeral? I could play it on the trombone." They all agreed it felt right.

"I would like to say a few words at the service but I'm not sure how that would be accepted." Linda wanted to draw a word picture of what she remembered about her sister and brother-in-law's lives. So her nieces told the minister that their Aunt Linda would say a few words.

Nancy did not go to the funeral, "Honey, I just can't," she told her remaining daughter.

The church was full of people. Linda began, "When Jean was small, she was a very determined little thing. Once, when she misbehaved, our mother sat her in a chair and said she would have to sit there until she was sorry. Mealtime came and bedtime and still she answered 'No!' when asked if she was sorry. She finally fell asleep in the chair." Linda did not talk about what life may have done to Jean's strong will.

"As you know, she was also very beautiful. When she grew up and I came along, I wanted to look just like her. I was in love with Jim Jeff when I was seven. The last time I came to Kansas City, Jean and I came to this church and stuck labels on envelopes because Jean volunteered here on Tuesdays mornings." The funeral was being held on a Tuesday.

Although Nancy Jones didn't say to Linda directly that she was proud of her, Linda overheard her say, "I don't know anyone else who could have stood up at her sister's funeral and spoken."

Since Linda's children were now all old enough to take care of themselves and, anyway, Michael was there with them, Linda stayed with her mother for a week after the funeral in her apartment. Any room could have been photographed for a magazine. They were filled with Aunt Georgia's antiques and kept spotless by Cleo who still worked for Nancy Jones after all of these years. Linda strolled the grounds, crossed a little bridge and walked along the stream where geese and swans floated and peacocks preened, believing themselves the owners of all they surveyed. It was all so beautiful and planned. Linda and Jean, with their word games, had dubbed it the Mansion Medical, because everyone who lived there was of a certain age.

She received a lovely note from Marcella who felt that she had failed her mother because she was not home when the news came.

For the first time in her life Linda wasn't the little sister. She couldn't pick up the phone and call Jean ever again. Kansas City was so lonely.

Chapter Twenty Seven

Linda and Cynthia giggled conspiratorially as they tried to spread the paint on the podiums in the cold gallery. It was all so totally ridiculous, trying to spread paint, or even stay in the cold unheated gallery. Winter was coming and the only warmth came from a small space heater. Linda figured, "If I stay here in the gallery and people keep coming, then they'll see that it should be open all year and they'll heat it."

Cynthia was shocked at some of the working conditions that Linda endured. She wrote a letter to Linda's boss and shook a figurative finger at the injustices.

Dear Ms. Dawson,

I am writing on behalf of Linda Jones with whom I have worked as a volunteer over the past several months at the River Cliffs Park Gallery. Linda loves the park and more than that, she has demonstrated that she does. She handles all the various aspects of her job honestly and competently, is unfailingly courteous with the public and has instituted order out of chaos. This, of course, is what she is paid to do; the point is that she does it exceptionally well, even in a building which is unheated during the winter...

Sincerely,
Cynthia Black

It was a beautiful letter; Linda was truly touched and, as a result, some of the conditions improved. Heat was installed in the tower.

"Thank you for writing, Cynthia. You know, I feel like I

keep meeting my mom at work, this vague feeling that I am a child and all of the other women are adults. I don't understand it."

Linda continued,"My supervisor says I can try to earn more money by starting a program for handicapped children or a folk dancing series in the ballroom. It was a couple of days before I thought of answering her by saying 'you mean making this gallery out of nothing only wins me the right to keep on keeping on'?"

"Did you tell her that?"

"Nope."

"I remember how much I enjoyed dancing with my boyfriend Wes when I was a teenager, so I told her I would work on the dances because it seems like something I know about and can do."

"I like to dance too, Linda; can I help you with the dances?"

The ballroom sat empty most of the time. It was used during one week of the year for an art show, and from time to time, for a dance. In preparation for the upcoming dance series she was arranging, Linda called and lined up bands and groups to teach different traditional kinds of dancing: square, contra, Irish, Israeli, while operating the gallery.

At first there were small crowds for the dances, but traditional dancing was enjoying a resurgence with the post-college crowd. Linda decided that now that they weren't in open revolt, they had energy to do something different and turned to dancing.

Cynthia and Linda ran brooms over the floor, greeted the bands, collected the money and took turns dancing. One night there was a Renaissance dance. Couples in costume swept regally down the hall and one could almost feel five hundred years had fallen away. One of the more irrepressible park rangers dressed as a gargoyle and crouched motionless on a balcony surveying the scene below. Linda thought to herself,

"I'll stay here forever; how could I ever leave the park?"

At midnight, when the lords and ladies had gone, Linda turned off the lights, crossed the dark ballroom and locked the door. As she was going down the hill towards the parking lot, she heard an eerie yell and turned back to the ballroom roof to see, silhouetted against the sky, the outline of the gargoyle calling to the moon.

The park was so central to her life that, at home when the phone rang and Linda absent-mindedly answered "River Cliffs Park, may I help you?" the girls laughed. Michael had accepted her every Saturday night obligation with characteristic stoicism.

With just two children at home now, she could try a little more successfully to help them with their own lives. Carroll, who had trouble learning in public school, came to her with a brochure about an alternative school and said, "Hey, Mom, I want to go to this school."

When she saw the price tag of $5,500 a year, Linda quietly filed it away. But Carroll came back and insisted, "I want to go to that school!"

Linda asked her mother for some money, arranged with Freddy to pay his monthly child support straight to the school and said to Michael, "I'm going to try to make her wish come true; will you take a bigger share of the home expenses?"

His mouth fell open at the price tag, "We can't afford this school," but he agreed to pay more of their living expenses.

"This school embodies some of the best from the 1960s and 70s revolution against establishment by concentrating on the individual and de-emphasizing meaningless rules," the director explained during the school admission interview.

Each youngster was part of a small tutorial that met twice a day and shared everything—if your parents fought, if you felt stupid or ugly, what it meant to be in foster care and move from home to home, or hungry because your mother didn't have any money. The school had scholarship students from the inner city. It was a good place for Carroll to share, "How would you like it if your mother had been married hundreds of times?"

Linda felt sad that she had been unable to do this for her other children, all of whom had had trouble in public school.

After Carroll had attended the school for a few weeks, she and Linda were sitting at the breakfast table alone one morning when Linda asked, "Why do you think this school is so good for you?"

Carroll answered, "Because you can talk to the teachers."

◆ ◆ ◆

Michael and Linda had lived together now for three years. He gave her a ring and they began to make plans to marry. At first, Linda felt like a very quiet private ceremony would be all she could stand. "Could we get married in a closet?" she joked. How could anyone believe her if she promised, again, "till death do us part"?

But Michael said, "I want to invite people from The Way."

Linda answered "Well, if you're going to invite them, then I'm going to invite my friends from the park," and the list grew.

When Michael asked her about a certain date in June, she answered "That's the festival at the Park."

Michael answered, "Linda!" but they didn't plan it that weekend.

There wasn't much money. Linda said, "I don't want to put us in more debt." So they decided on a party in their yard and they asked their guests to bring a dish to share. Michael borrowed and strung up colorful parachutes from the trees and his parents brought in a cake that was made in the country. His brothers couldn't come; they were making hay.

Linda's mother didn't come. She said, "Oh, Honey, I can't travel anymore." The wedding happened to be scheduled for the day after Nancy Jones turned 78.

Linda wrote her nieces and said, "You'd better come; I might not get a fourth offer."

Their backdoor neighbors donated the services of a pianist and they moved the piano out on the front porch. All in all, it was a lovely day. Linda got a mischievous look on her face and told Michael, "It was the loveliest wedding I have ever had." They even went on a honeymoon.

Chapter Twenty Eight

Linda had worked at the park for ten years, explaining to the public when they asked, "Why is this park falling down?"

"The service didn't get the deed until 1976...the park has been on the list to work on the old buildings, but the budget deficit..." Then she heard a speech about "What the Private Sector Can Accomplish" and decided during those twenty minutes that was what she would do: she would start an organization to raise money to save her beloved park. Linda began to read everything she could get her hands on about nonprofit organizations that raise funds for a cause.

Linda went to her boss and announced, "Next spring, I am going to leave the park service and go to work for an organization to raise money for the park."

Linda also was working on another project; she and Michael were actively trying to get pregnant. They had been married for a couple of years and, although they didn't use birth control, she was not pregnant.

"It's not surprising," said her doctor, "in a woman your age." He went on to give her the name of a couple of fertility experts, although he told her that he didn't really approve of her getting pregnant.

When Linda called the first doctor's office they said they didn't accept women over forty for treatment but she was able to get an appointment with the second doctor.

He said, "I'm not terribly optimistic but we'll give Pergonal three months try."

So every morning before she went to work, Linda went to

his office to get a shot and have blood drawn on alternate visits. The nurses were amused by Linda coming in her uniform and dropping her trousers for the treatment.

"Isn't it too bad?" the nurse said to Linda after a couple of weeks worth of visits.

Linda, who had no idea what she was talking about, asked "What's too bad?"

"Well, your hormone count is only up to fifty."

"What's it supposed to be up to?"

"Ideally, to get pregnant, it should be around a thousand."

April, 1985

Dear Marie,

You won't believe this but I am pregnant again, at age 47. I have wanted this one last baby for a long time. It surprised even the fertility expert. The baby is due in the fall.

I am going to Kansas City to visit Mom next week and tell her I am expecting.

Love,
Linda

Dear Linda,
WHAT?

Love,
Marie

"Oh no, Honey, it's just the change," said Nancy.

"No, Mama, I've been to the doctor and had a test."

Nancy said, "Well, I don't know what I would have done without my children. Sometimes I think I tried to make you too perfect. I'll just hang on until that baby comes. " She had said she wanted to die for several years now.

Nancy, who was 81, had recently cut back from two packs of cigarettes a day to one when her doctor said, "Mrs. Jones, you are suffering from emphysema."

But nothing made her cut down on the whiskey.

When the month of May came along, Linda was put to bed because the doctor feared she might lose the pregnancy, due to "an incompetent cervix." Of course he knew about the baby she had lost and how Andy was almost born early.

Feelings raged in her body because, on the one hand, she did want to be pregnant, but she had become accustomed to moving about in the world, having opportunities to use her brain and her creativity. All of a sudden she wasn't supposed to use her anything.

Just the night before she was abruptly sent to bed, she had opened a show in the gallery with the theater company. Her first day in bed, the carousel operator called her with a question, she felt so frustrated to not be able to go and help that she slammed her fist through the wall. She knew that everyone would forget her; she would lose her place in the world. She and Michael also feared that they wouldn't end up with a baby. She longed to talk. Michael, never very talkative, would come home in the evenings eager to relax. One evening, as he was taking off his coat and tie, Linda yelled, "Say something!" Perplexed, Michael just looked at her in anguish, as if words and emotions were tumbling around in his head, unable to come out of his mouth. Linda felt terrible because she yelled; Michael felt terrible because he couldn't say the right thing.

Michael bought a VCR machine; he had been wanting one and now it seemed to him that he had an excuse and they began to watch horror movies. The movies were good lightening rods for all of the anxiety in the house.

Carroll, who was graduating from high school that spring, called her mother the "beached whale." It was disturbing and embarrassing to see her mother flat in bed, not upright, strong and confident.

Linda made some rules for herself, since she was going to have to stay in bed: no television or reading that didn't have redeeming factors. Cynthia brought her all the Bronte books and she began to read. She lay on her back and fringed four blue and white napkins for Natasha's birthday. Also, she read about raising funds and nonprofit organizations. It was hard to keep on believing that she would get the opportunity to raise money for the park but it was hard to believe anything right then.

The month went by and they went in for a sonogram. This doctor, a comic and the mentor for her own obstetrician, told them, "You're expecting a girl. You don't have an incompetent cervix, you have an incompetent doctor!" and suddenly it was okay for her to get up.

But Linda was more accustomed now to just living and gestating, so she resumed life upright but didn't go back to work at the park. She had never taken sick leave, so she had enough leave to be paid for the rest of the pregnancy. She exercised to Jane Fonda's workout tape for pregnant women, made some fabric art, chaired the town's annual crabfeast, and delivered a healthy girl in November, 1985.

This delivery was so different from that of her first baby girl, twenty-five years before. Linda and Michael had gone to birthing class together beforehand. The group sat in a circle and introduced themselves, "Hi, I'm John; this is my wife Marcia and this is our first baby..." from all ten couples. Until the last couple, Michael and Linda, when Michael introduced them "I'm Michael and this is my wife Linda. This is my first baby and her...sixth."

Everyone learned to breathe, to pant, to breast-feed. Linda knew very well how to nurse a baby but she wanted the whole experience to be shared with Michael.

All of the other mothers in class had delivered their babies and the doctor finally decided to take Linda's baby by Caesarian delivery when Linda hadn't gone into labor two weeks past due date. There was never any question that Michael would be there for the baby's arrival and Linda and

Michael held hands on one side of the sheet that ran across her midsection. The only blood and gore they saw was in a tube than ran up from behind the sheet. Linda said, rather nonchalantly, "It might as well be someone else's blood." After the baby was delivered, Michael was excited and torn between wanting to be with the baby and with Linda. When they wheeled the baby out of the delivery room, Linda told him, "Go with the baby."

Linda was waiting in recovery alone when Natasha arrived with a bouquet of flowers she had picked. "Hi, how did you get in here? Michael has gone off with the baby; I'm so glad you're here."

Natasha had designed, drawn, painted, and given them birth announcements with a rosy-cheeked baby kicking on the front.

When she was wheeled to her room, Linda picked up the phone and tried to call her mother and tell her that the baby had arrived but there was no answer to her call. "That's strange," thought Linda. She knew her mother never went anywhere now. Linda called her nieces and cousin to see if anyone knew anything. They all said Nancy had been sick for a while.

Finally three days after the birth, her mother answered the phone, sounding weak. The conversation was pretty unsatisfactory; Linda could barely hear her mother. She couldn't tell what her mother was saying, but at least she knew she was alive. Nancy said, "I'm going to call 911 on Saturday and go to the hospital."

"Mama, that's not the way you do it," Linda answered. But that's the way her mother did it.

Saturday when Linda and the baby came home, Nancy called 911 and went into the hospital. After she was better, the doctors would not allow Nancy to return home alone. They were afraid she would return to drinking every day again and be unable to care for herself. She went instead to a nursing home.

Although the baby had been born in November, before Christmas Nancy called Linda and asked, "Please come help me get out of the nursing home."

Linda answered, "Mama, if I come there now with a new baby, right before Christmas, with four older kids coming here, I'll lose my mind."

And she didn't go, even when they called her right before Christmas to tell her that, "Your mother has fallen and hit her head."

Jean and Jim Jeff's oldest daughter oversaw her grandmother's care and it was not until early in the new year that Linda, Michael, the new baby and Heather drove out to Kansas City. Marcella called from the west coast to see if she should come. "I don't think you need to come. I'll call you if you need to," Linda told her. Marcella came anyway.

They arrived at the nursing home and Linda ran to her mother's room but the bed was empty.

"Where's my mother?" she asked the nurse. Nancy had been returned to the hospital; she had a relapse. So they all went to the hospital and sneaked the baby past the nurses' station.

They found Nancy barely conscious but her first question was "Where's that baby?"

When they showed her the baby, she said "This one'll be a model; she's the best looking yet." Nancy Jones' wish for any female born into the family was to be beautiful; brains were for the boys. It seemed to work too. All of the women in the family were beautiful. None of them seemed surer of themselves because of it.

Nancy had gotten the idea that the true measure of femininity lay in the size of hands and feet. She had always insisted, "Linda has such tiny little hands and feet." By that measure then, Linda should have felt pretty sure of her womanhood.

One day when she was sixteen and walking through their mother's bedroom, Jean had said, "Mom, look what a big rear Linda has!" After that they were even. Jean had big feet but Linda had big hips.

It was difficult to be a woman in this family. Linda had felt inferior when she went back to Kansas for a visit and went to the department store with Jean. They would browse through the racks. Jean had always been sure of her own taste. Linda considered Jean's and her mother's taste to be perfect and her own to be wobbly. She would try pulling a dress from the rack and saying something favorable.

Usually, Jean would answer, "Do you really like that?" and Linda would hastily answer that she didn't, of course not. But that left her unsure what she was supposed to like.

After a week visiting Nancy in Kansas City, everyone else went back to their lives and Linda and the baby stayed in her mother's apartment to move out and close up. Nancy was back in the nursing home and every day Linda went to visit her mother, carrying things she thought might make it easier for her mother to stay there. Linda chose an antique painting on porcelain with a heavy gilt frame and her mother's Hitchcock rocking chair. Carting the baby and the chair, the baby and the frame, the diaper bag and her purse, in and out from the car to the nursing home, she was trying to please her mother. There was little conversation. Sometimes, Nancy was barely aware and Linda just dutifully sat there. Once, when the baby cried out, Nancy said, "Oh hush!"

In addition to going back and forth to the nursing home every day, she was making the racking decisions involved in choosing what would go into storage in case her mother was able to resume assisted living in a smaller place.

Ghosts of the past came out of every drawer as she opened it alone. Linda kept the case of Johnny Walker Red Label by the front door and gave out bottles as door favors to her nephew, nieces, cousin, aunt, assorted visitors.

One morning as she was sitting in her mother's kitchen eating eggs and bacon alone while the baby was still sleeping,

Linda reached over and turned on the television. A voice was telling how the Challenger was ready for lift off. The count down came and the spaceship lifted off, rose in the air and seemed to...fall apart. Linda was unsure what was happening. There was no one else around to check her perceptions. The reality—watching seven lives being snuffed out in an instant —was too terrible to contemplate. Linda had to hear it on the radio again on the way to the nursing home to digest the fact. It was January 28, 1986.

When she arrived at the nursing home, her mother, who hadn't said much else for days, said, "Wasn't it awful, what happened to those young astronauts?" It seemed to Linda that her mother was unconscious to her, but not to the world.

Four times that year, she went back and forth to Kansas City with her baby, on and off the plane, in and out of the rental cars, carrying baby, bags, stroller. Sometimes Nancy was better, one time even well enough to leave the new nursing home where Linda's niece, Debbie, had moved her. Linda and her mother went to Debbie's for dinner. Nancy was excep-tionally sweet during the evening and only winced, but said nothing, when she saw her porcelain painting in the gilt frame, lying flat on Debbie's buffet, with things piled on the fragile frame. At the nursing home, Nancy had said to Debbie, "Get the rocking chair and that painting out of here." Nancy had not wanted the nursing home to seem like home.

The next day's visit after the pleasant dinner in Debbie's home was different, however. When Linda arrived, her mother was waiting to pounce on her, "Why did you give my mother's soup tureen to my sister?"

Linda started to answer, "But she was her mother..." This wasn't supposed to be a two-way conversation, not according to Nancy's rules. It was an opportunity for her to express anger at her daughter for the twist life had taken yet both of them believed Nancy was angry with Linda.

In her frustration, Linda decided that this time she would

make her mother hear her. This would be a two-way conversation, and Linda put one hand on each of the wheelchair's handles and leaned toward her mother, starting to yell, "You listen to me!" She didn't care if they kicked her out of the nursing home. This time her mother would hear her if it was the last thing she did.

But her mother didn't hear her. Linda finally realized that and quit yelling, quit trying to talk at all. She had often felt that way with her mother—wordless. When she did, she reminded herself, rather harshly, of Red Skelton's character, Willy Lump-lump, not very bright, not knowing what to say.

Linda pushed her mother's wheelchair to the dining room at lunchtime and sat silently until she had a thought. "It must be really hard to lose your home?"

Nancy Jones nodded, with tears in her eyes.

Nancy had always said, "I hope I can live alone until I die."

That fall on her baby's first birthday, Linda received a call from Debbie, "Aunt Linda, you better come."

When Linda arrived at the hospital and pushed the stroller into her mother's room, her mother said, "Where did you get those earrings?"

Linda thought to herself "This dame isn't dying."

Marcella came again and ministered to her grandmother lovingly, with all of the little things that she learned to do as a nurse. On the fourth day though, she had to leave, but not before she said to her mother, "Gram only has a few days at the most to live."

Linda made up her mind that she would spend as much of the remaining time as possible at her mother's side. She drove Marcella into Kansas City to the airport, with the baby in her car seat in the back. On the way back out to the nursing home, driving across the Kansas farm lands, Linda had the sudden impulse to turn down the radio—out of respect. Pictures passed before her eyes of her parents' lives over the years, set there in the great plains, the little house in Grain

Valley with her mother as a young woman seated on the front steps, her dad in the Model T holding her sister as a baby, the fields and fields of growing things where city people came in the late 1930s to sleep in gullies by the road because there was no relief from the heat in the cities.

When she arrived at the hospital and asked about her mother, the nurses looked almost guilty, and she knew then that they would have to tell her that her mother was dead, had just died fifteen minutes before. Linda felt like apologizing to the nurses and saying, "It's all right, don't worry, my mother and I weren't normal; I don't have to have her."

But instead, she asked to go in and she said, in an almost formal manner to her mother's body, "I'm sorry, good-bye, I love you," even though she was never sure about that.

Chapter Twenty Nine

In the spring, the park service unwittingly went along with Linda's plan to form an organization to raise money for the park by announcing that the money needed to fix the River Cliffs buildings would not be forthcoming. They had already condemned and destroyed a couple of the buildings.

Linda and Michael and the baby were on the west coast visiting Marcella and Carroll, who had also moved there to attend college. "Ma, the phone's for you," Marcella said as she handed it over.

"Hi, Linda, sorry to bother you but I know you would want to hear that the park service's putting the park up for rent," Cynthia called with the news. "There's going to be a meeting at the Sullivan's next week to plan a way to save the park, will you be back in time?"

Linda said, "Sure, I'll be there. I wouldn't miss it!"

There were about 30 people at the little meeting in the Sullivans' living room and they decided the thing to do was plan a bigger meeting in the Town Hall and attract more people and media attention.

Linda wrote a press release on the used electric typewriter she had bought years before for $25. When the children were small, she needed to hide in the bathroom to write. She sat on the floor and put the typewriter on the toilet seat and told the children to disturb her only if it was an absolute emergency. Every "emergency" was subject to scrutiny.

First came the knock on the bathroom door.

"What do you want?"

"Heather's teasing me."

"Go away from her."

"I can't. There's nothing else to do."

"I'll find some work for you to do," Linda's stock answer to any kid who had nothing to do. It was the end of the emergency.

Linda had kept her tenuous hold on sanity that way. Nancy Jones had said, "That's what you should do, Linda; you should be a writer." Linda thought wryly to herself that she could have used this message a little earlier.

During her ranger days at River Cliffs, she had learned to do press releases and thanks to her efforts, the park had received a fair amount of attention from the media.

Now, the little frame town hall was so crowded that some people had to be turned away. Television crews recorded the evening's events and ran them on the late news.

Several people spoke, Linda among them. She told about all of the wonderful activities that went on at the park—the art, the wonderful 1920s carousel, dancing in the ballroom—and said, "That's not the end of all this at the park...yet!"

Energy built up in the crowd; people were donating money and volunteering. Linda dreamt of devoting the rest of her life to saving River Cliffs Park. In her fantasy of retiring someday, she was grey-haired and lauded for what she had accomplished.

After the big meeting, Linda worked as a volunteer, with the baby on her hip, to build the organization. There were plenty of calls—from the owner of an alternative radio station, from wealthy businessmen. Michael was impressed. When baby Codey started to fuss, Linda plugged her into her breast. It was important to sound businesslike, something not possible with a crying baby in your arms.

Natasha, whose art was used to illustrate brochures for the park, designed a logo and posters for the foundation. Natasha's work said, "River Cliffs Park" without words. She had been an artist at the park since the earliest days when, during the free-wheeling seventies, young people with grand visions from both the service and the artistic community begged, borrowed or took whatever the park needed to survive. In fact, at park service headquarters, whenever they saw the River Cliffs park manager arriving with his cohort, they said "Here come those crooks."

Later, the bureaucracy had imposed itself on the age of Aquarius at River Cliffs Park, but not without a struggle. For Linda, it began with the first park manager, a little African American woman who drove a big motorcycle, who said, "You have to start wearing a uniform."

"A uniform?" Linda had asked in disbelief.

In getting the park into orthodox shape, the service killed some of the original community feeling, but this fight to save the park brought back a sense of connection. People came from every direction: artists whose lives were invested in the park, everyday people who studied at the park, people who had met their spouses fifty years ago in the ballroom.

Linda threw herself into unpaid, forty or more hour weeks organizing, writing, meeting. Fortuitously, a big circus had come to town and parked on the parking lot at the park. They offered one of their performances as a fundraiser. It just happened that a friend with whom Linda had gone to college in Missouri knew one of the ex-owners of the circus and connected Linda up with him. Through him, Linda was able to get a special deal to buy tickets for a benefit performance and the foundation made $10,000 from the circus fundraiser.

◆ ◆ ◆

For years, Linda had written to Cleo, asking her, "Why don't you come back here for a visit and see the nation's capital?"

Nancy Jones had promised to leave money for Cleo when

she died. Nancy enjoyed giving so much that she sometimes gave the same thing to more than one person, like promising her silver to more than one grandchild or saying she would leave someone money in her will but she didn't. Linda didn't have the heart to tell Cleo the truth and she felt like Cleo deserved something for all of her years of work, so she told her that they would have to wait until probate settled everything. Then Linda made arrangements that several thousand would go to Cleo, who decided to really come now that she had a little money.

Linda went to the airport with the baby and waited as the Kansas City passengers deplaned. She watched as the tall black woman came round the corner in a lime green polyester travel suit. She is amazing, thought Linda. Cleo was the same age as her mother had been and was still going strong. Of course, the wig helped to belie the 80-plus years.

Cleo stayed for a week and slept in the baby's room because theirs was still a two-bedroom house. She went wherever Linda went, met her friends. When she went with Linda to the park, Linda smiled to herself because it looked to her as if people were going out of their way to greet Cleo. Linda imagined they were thinking Cleo must really be somebody important. Else why was this tall, black, self-possessed elderly woman here, now?

It was hard to integrate someone from a different generation and race into their own life. Michael loved the privacy of his home; it was almost beyond him. When he didn't say much to her, Cleo asked, "Why doesn't Michael like me?" Michael tried; he went out and rented the video *Out of Africa* for Linda and Cleo to watch one evening. He thought it might be something Cleo would enjoy.

One day Linda drove downtown to show Cleo the Capital and monuments. It ended up a tour from the car since one couldn't park near any of the sights and it would have been a strain for Cleo to walk the distances required. "There's the

Jefferson Memorial and the tidal basin...along here on both sides are different buildings of the Smithsonian."

When Cleo left, she asked Linda to write down all of the names of the people she had met.

"Do you want their addresses? Are you going to write them letters?" Linda asked. Cleo had only gone to school a few years in her Texas childhood, but she had written Linda at least once a year since Linda left home many years before. Linda loved receiving the letters although they were a challenge to read.

"No, I don't think so," said Cleo; she just wanted to know who she knew. They would probably became beneficiaries of Cleo's prayers back in Kansas City, Linda thought to herself.

Chapter Thirty

It was a large and diverse group of people who had assembled themselves as the board of directors of the park friends' group. They sat around a long table and the ones who knew the least tried to look like they knew it all. There was quite a task before them and some thought their most valuable contribution would be good advice.

"That's okay, Linda, you can do the work," Elizabeth chuckled.

Elizabeth had been telling Linda for years, "The service is going to do the same thing to River Cliffs that they did to Quail Creek; they are going to close it when they run out of money."

Now that events had proven that Elizabeth was right, she wanted to be there to see it unfold so she had joined the board. With her soft, pleasant Richmond accent, she could calmly predict from her own experience what to expect. Everyone on the board thought Elizabeth's advice was excellent.

Sometimes, after the meetings, Linda, Natasha, Cynthia and Elizabeth went out and had a few laughs at the expense of the stuffed shirts. At the corner of the park there was an old frame building that had been a road house and now was reconstituted as a chic new restaurant and bar. Linda's better self said she shouldn't laugh; there would be some price to pay but it was satisfying.

Linda had told the board several times that she wanted to work for them when they were ready to hire staff, but they seemed to have little appreciation for her offer. She knew the park and the service from the inside like no one else. Looking back later, she would realize it would have been difficult for them to appreciate her when she didn't fully appreciate herself.

It came as a shock one night when Linda entered the board meeting a few minutes late and heard them interviewing someone else for a paid position. They hired the woman that evening, but she hadn't been involved in the initial planning and didn't know what needed to be done, without someone telling her. Linda kept her mouth shut. When the new employee asked, "What needs to be done?"

Some board members answered, "You better find out!"

After a month or so, the woman left and Linda breathed a little easier, thinking that now the board would understand how much she herself was needed.

Elizabeth tried to help Linda position herself. She cautioned Linda, "Now just keep your mouth shut and let me do the talking, okay? Let's sort of pretend to not be close friends. I can find out what's going on if they don't associate me with you." She knew that Linda would lay all of her cards out on the table. This way, Elizabeth could act on Linda's behalf without anyone else realizing. Unfortunately, that also kept them from realizing that Elizabeth, with all of her good advice, was involved because of her connection to Linda.

Several months later, at a board meeting, Elizabeth said, "Our projects are too numerous and complicated; we need a paid staff." A committee wrote a job description and advertised in the newspaper. They allowed Linda to apply, along with several others, to do what she'd been doing for free. The evening set aside for interviews, Linda arrived early, feeling confident. She started into the park office.

"Wait outside please," one of the committee asked. Linda was embarrassed by her own enthusiasm. When it was her turn, she was able to answer their questions, after all she had been thinking and reading about this for years.

The hiring committee came to the conclusion that Linda knew more about the park and the job than the other applicants and hired her. She had asked the committee if she could work part-time but they had said, "Absolutely not; you need to be here full time."

Codey was two and Linda wanted Michael to help her find day care for the toddler while she was working. He said, "We wouldn't have this problem if you didn't want to go back to work."

But she said, "Wrong, we wouldn't have this problem if we didn't have a baby. Do you remember how worried you were about making ends meet when I resigned my position right before she was born?" She thought of how guilty she would have felt twenty years before, trying to do what she wanted to do. She also knew that she probably wouldn't have been able to stand up for herself so well with a husband her own age.

Her older friends said, "Why are you going back to work when your baby is only two years old?"

But younger women said, "Aren't you lucky; you were able to stay home with your baby for two years!"

They could not have afforded day care if her mother had not died and left money. Because Codey was still in diapers, it cost $320 every two weeks, plus 64 disposable diapers every month, not to mention a $479 materials fee for the year. Her parents' money had shrunk from a lifetime guarantee to a little something that made a few luxuries possible for a while, like being able to accept the job she wanted. Nonetheless, Linda often said in her mind, "Thanks, Mom and Dad, for making this possible."

Linda found a day care center close enough to home so that she could put Codey in her seat on the back of the bicycle and ride her to care and herself to work.

On her fiftieth birthday she threw a big party at the restaurant close to the park and invited all of her friends. Linda and Natasha found a tabloid newspaper front page with a headline "Mother, 50, Hasn't Aged Since 18!" With a few changes, a reprint made a perfect birthday party invitation. Linda planned the party with great food and champagne and spared few expenses, another one of those luxuries she never would have been able to afford without her parents' money.

Chapter Thirty One

Linda had to watch herself. She was tempted to stay late, work weekends and evenings. There was so much to do and it was exciting! She was down to the last two days of writing a grant request for $50,000 and had the papers spread out on two tables in her office, going over the attachments. Michael called to say, "I picked Codey up from day care and she has a temperature and is fussy."

"Okay, I'll be home, just give me another half hour. Give her a painkiller, the purple ones in the medicine cabinet, and rock her until I get there."

Linda hurried to get the packet, all sixteen copies, in order with three sets of multiple page attachments. She could call the messenger service in the morning, but what if Codey was still ill in the morning? Well, she would just have to bring her down to the park until this proposal was out the door.

Some nights, after dinner, she was back in her office; her eyes felt like they needed toothpicks to stay open.

And then, after a couple of months, "Cynthia! We won the $50,000 grant!" Linda almost screamed into the phone. The letter had arrived with the congratulatory greeting and the pages of cautions and required financial reports and deadlines.

This and the good results of the first few direct mailings and they were on the way.

May, 1988

Dear Marie,
These few months have been very busy and satisfying. My mind

feels like it's full of ends that I am tying together. At last I have a job that uses my talents and satisfies me. One day at work the phone rang and an older woman said her name was Mrs. Einstein and her father used to manage the amusement park. I remembered her father's name since I knew the park's history. She was impressed that I knew and she decided to ask her friends and family to make contributions to the park instead of gifts for her 75th birthday. I practically caused a double car crash when I drove past the Jewish Community Association later and saw a large sign with the words, "Sydney Einstein Construction Company." So apparently Mrs. Einstein really has money. Hopefully all this will fit together to bring in the what the park needs.

Codey and Michael are fine.

Love,
Linda

As she walked across the park during the $50,000 celebration, she realized that most of the people she saw knew her and Linda made every effort to call them by name and say a few words with them. She chuckled to herself, "This is almost like being a politician."

Chapter Thirty Two

The board was struggling to choose a new chairman but when Cynthia told Linda, "I think I might like to be chairman," Linda was absolutely delighted. It would be such fun to work together.

It wasn't difficult to convince the board to accept Cynthia's offer because few of them really wanted to spend the time that chairmanship would take, so Cynthia invited Linda to lunch to celebrate her coming election.

As they sat waiting for their order, she showed Linda a stack of drawings, saying "These are stories and illustrations for a children's book. I did them. I showed these to my sister and then this book came out." Cynthia pulled out a charming little book that had her sister's name as author. "She stole my idea. This is what is probably going to happen to you at the park; you are never going to get credit for what you have done."

It was a thought-provoking lunch, but Linda didn't really believe that would happen. "No one would get rid of me when I work so hard for the park," she said.

She had forgotten Adriane Hanrahan's saying, many years before, "People aren't rational beings." At the time, Linda couldn't imagine what Adriane was talking about.

There was really no contest and at the next board meeting, they elected Cynthia as the new chairman.

As soon as the election was over, Cynthia stood before the board and announced, "I can't do this job unless we hire a professional fundraiser."

Linda almost stopped breathing, afraid she would betray herself if she took a deep breath. This was a complete surprise. It was the beginning of the nightmare, a waking nightmare. Linda's hands almost trembled as she gathered up papers and cleaned up from the meeting while little groups of directors gathered and buzzed around her.

Cynthia said, "I intend to come in for lunch tomorrow; we need to talk." They ate lunch together again, but not at the fancy restaurant. This time, they met in one of the basement rooms at the park. Cynthia turned to her and said, "We have been friends, but now our relationship will change; I am your boss."

Linda felt like she had no intention of challenging Cynthia but wondered why Cynthia thought it had to be this way.

That evening Linda told Michael, "So much could be taken away from me, almost everything important in life. What if I lost my place at the park?"

"What makes you think you might?" Michael asked.

"Well, they can't afford to pay a professional fundraiser and me. I should know; I raised the money. And Cynthia has become absolutely imperious. She scares me and she knows it. I feel like I'm on the edge of falling down the hole in *Alice in Wonderland*."

It was hard for Linda to sleep most nights past the first two hours. She awoke to mull over everything that needed to be done. It was much harder under a cloud of fear.

Most of the time, Linda tried to do what Cynthia wanted, but she came up with ideas that seemed crazy to Linda. When Linda stalled for time to try to think them out, Cynthia came charging into the office and shouted, "I know you! If you had wanted to do that, it would have been done yesterday!" Secretly, Linda was pleased at the compliment. The summer was spent on the search for a professional fundraiser in answer to Cynthia's request. Proposals arrived and Linda read through them, making copies for the committee.

The firm was chosen in August. Linda sat in on their interview. They talked in seeming professional terms "about a possible involvement of the Masons in raising money for the park..."

One day that fall, Cynthia came in and ordered Linda, "Follow me out to the picnic area." They sat facing each other and Cynthia said, as if she were speaking to someone who was not very bright, "I want you to send this agenda packet to all of the board without reading it; do you understand? You will not be welcome at this meeting."

There had never been a board meeting without Linda. She was stunned. The weeks went by, and at the November meeting, Cynthia pointed out to the board members, "We cannot continue to pay both the fundraising firm and Linda."

The board decided since there wasn't money for both, Linda's position was to be abolished at the end of the year. Several members of the board walked out of the meeting and resigned, but no one stood up for her, at least not successfully. Maybe they would have, had Linda been there to lead the charge but she just couldn't do it.

"I suspected something fishy, but I wasn't sure, so I just left," one of her allies told Linda. "I never did like that woman."

Chapter Thirty Three

In a way, this was slightly better. Now there was no fear; the worst had happened.

"Sadness isn't quite as paralyzing as fear," Linda wrote Marie. "I'm making photocopies of everything we accomplished. Partly I tell myself it's pointless but I do it anyway."

Near the end of the year, the chosen professional fundraising firm sent out a young woman who was to be their staff person at the park. She was chewing gum, which she kept poking back into her mouth with a multi-ringed finger, as she listened to Linda telling her what was in the files. "I hope they don't expect me to stay out here all of the time," the young woman said to no one in particular.

At the end of the year, Linda's friends threw her a "retirement" party and she was glad that she could decline the rather feeble offer that the board made. "No thank you; you don't need to have a party." she was able to say, "It would just be a duplication of efforts."

Chapter Thirty Four

When 1990 and the job were all over, Linda called Elizabeth and asked, "Could I list the farm as one of the places I searched for a job when I fill out the unemployment form?" Linda thought she would just sit home for a long time and draw unemployment compensation as a revenge to the foundation board. She was angry, furious in fact, and so painfully hurt. And she felt almost, but not quite, empty.

She could hardly stand it when the next River Cliffs Park Foundation newsletter arrived in the mail, addressed to "Mr. and Mrs. Michael Tanner" and never even mentioned that she was gone, involuntarily removed from the scene. After six years of her life given to the park, or fifteen depending on how you looked at it, nothing was said about her at all. But the state required a person drawing unemployment to look for work; they wouldn't let anyone sit home to nurse their wounds. Linda ran out of friends to list as pretend job interviewers; she had to go on a real job interview. For the first time she asked herself, "What would I like to do?" That was one small step. Every job she had had before came along and found her, or it had seemed that way.

As Linda drove around the beltway, she envisioned doing something for people; the idea was vague, a little like the one she had as a teenager when she applied to Henry Street Settlement House in New York. Only now, her father wasn't there to say anything about it.

Linda looked in the newspaper and saw an opening that

looked interesting and the first place she applied, she was offered a job working for a small nonprofit that raised money for foster children.

Michael said "It's not supposed to happen like that; you're not supposed to get the first job you try for," but it did. Linda found that all of the things she had learned to do for her beloved park could be applied elsewhere and were, indeed, saleable skills.

For the rest of her life, Linda would feel, whenever she heard of someone losing an election, losing a position suddenly which meant everything to them, she would say a silent prayer for them. She knew how it was. She remembered then coming home at age 16 and seeing her father's tears when his partners bought him out.

Some days, on her way to her new downtown job Linda would see people in uniforms working in the parks and it would remind her of River Cliffs Park. One day, the theater company drove past her on their way out to River Cliffs Park and she waved, but they didn't see her. She reminded herself as sternly as she could that hers was a different life now.

As Linda climbed the escalator from the subway, Linda felt she was still fighting through clouds of grief but, somehow, her feet went forward.

To order additional copies of *Crossing Kansas*, please fill out the order form, make check payable to Diane Leatherman, and send to: Diane Leatherman

   Box 315

   Cabin John, MD 20818-0315

   Telephone: 301-229-1524

Please send me

_____ total books (_____ copies at $10.95 per copy)

_____ tax (Maryland residents add 5% sales tax .55)

_____ shipping ($1.50 for first book, .25 each additional book)

_____ **TOTAL**